EMPIRE OF THE FIFTH SUN DIFICIL

STEVEN VALTIERRA

DEDICATION

I am proud to dedicate this story to our ancestors, the Azteca, with the hope I have given them the true respect and acknowledgment of their advanced intelligence, rich culture and "Oneness" with the earth and its inhabitants! I also dedicate this book to my own "Amazon," my wife Connie. I thank you for the countless hours and days you sat with me and listened and encouraged me to write this book; always giving me your most honest and critical opinion. You helped me sort out my ideas and you gave me the confidence to see this book to its completion.

ACKNOWLEDGMENTS

I would like to thank the Lord for providing me with the ability, patience and perseverance to write this book. Without His blessings, I would not have the basic tools to write.

INTRODUCTION

From atop the Great Pyramid, he looked upon his land, his Empire, his people.

The young prince had already experienced his baptism of war! He fought with tenacity, cunning and bravery!

"Dificil" is an exciting creature full of life, possessing many gifts and talents. He was an Azteca who demonstrated rare compassion and mercy and yet displayed great cunning and decisive actions to save his family and his kingdom. The description of his free, lively spirit and his love of all plants, animals and most of his fellow men exemplifies the true Azteca culture. This is someone who was taught and trained as the next Emperor, the next "Tlatoani" of the Azteca world. Dificil enjoyed children's play, humor, and hi-jinks just like any other young child of today, but at the same time, he had to grow up very fast! You will read of his sensitivities, his love and anger, but most of all, you will read of his being a gifted child, a child seemingly sent by the Gods themselves! Dificil, with his awesome strength, courage, and wisdom, will lead the Azteca into a harsh, difficult and dangerous era.

As a result of the victory over a southern tribe, Dificil meets the Amazon Queen Consuelo. He is enchanted by this beautiful, wild, creature who is full of fury and tenacity and the two become one!

His life will become legend, and his legacy will become the life of the Azteca!

Please read on and experience the world of "DIFICIL," the beginning of the era of the "Fifth Sun," the reign of the Azteca Empire, these former rulers of the world who, with their intelligence, inventions, and discoveries, lived in a golden age of creation and majesty.

CHAPTER ONE
"THE BIRTH OF A KING"

As she lay on her bed, she moaned and screamed at the top of her lungs, and then she fainted again! The Aztec Physicians were "Teopixque" (priest) and had delivered many babies before, but this was the very special birth of the "Pilli," (Nahuatl language meaning "Royal Son"), the firstborn of the Great Chichinotpotl, the ruler of all Aztecs and his Empress Cuicani! This was a most difficult delivery for the Queen; she was now so tired and weak, but they knew she must remain conscious or it would be very dangerous for both her and the not-yet-born "Pilli." All three different Aztec doctors were present because this was a royal birth. The "Teopati," (Aztec Doctors who treated physical symptoms), the "Tictli," (those seeking and addressing spiritual causes), and the "Tlametpatli," (the medical specialist who were experts in herbal medicine and who drew on their ancient healing art to treat problems including heart trouble, stomach sickness and breathing disorders). All the forms of mixed herbal remedies were prepared. All the Teopixque, present trembled in fear as the Empress Cuicani repeatedly shouted blasphemies of the gods as she squeezed the hand of her husband, the Great Emperor Chichinotpotl. He was valiantly trying to withstand the pain of his wife's fingernails digging into his skin! Even through suffering such great pains of childbirth, the Empress, with feigned humor, screamed, "It is your fault that

I lay here struggling and suffering from bearing this monstrosity of a child! I fear the gods are punishing me for past sins that I have committed! Why else would I have to carry such a huge load for nine months?" "Oh, my dearest flower petal, it seems our child is much larger than any other child born before on this earth. That is why I previously offered to have the NaNas (nannies) follow you around during your pregnancy to help you carry this wonderful package," Chichinotpotl said as he fought the urge to smile. The Empress screamed again as the horrified doctors urged her to keep pushing, as the baby was starting to finally come out. The senior Teopati, then began to stutter as he tried to communicate something to the emperor. "My L, L, L, Lo, Lord, I fear that there will be grave consequences if we do not apply an incision to help the Empress deliver this child! It is too big for her to release on her own!" With such an anxious, concerned look, Chichinotpotl said, "If you feel that you must, then proceed, but be extremely careful, for I hold you responsible for any mistakes that may cause injury to my wife or my child!"

As the physicians completed their calculated incision, they were further horrified because they could see that the baby was coming out feet first! A Breach birth! By the gods, this would be even more dangerous! The empress continued to push as the physicians pulled! Great Quetzalcoatl! He was finally completely out! The priest gasped as did the NaNas and Chichinotpotl when they saw how large the baby was! The Teopixque cleared his airway and massaged his back, then the baby spit out, screamed, and cried out loud! Everyone present seemed to take a deep breath of relief at the same time when they heard the baby cry because they knew then that he was alive! The Empress Cuicani smiled with large tears in her eyes as she looked upon her newborn son and clutched him close to her breast. Beaming with pride, she had instantly forgotten about all the pain she had endured delivering him. Maybe later she would even forgive her husband for causing her pregnancy with this "Monstrosity!" Upon further examination, the "Teopati" discovered that the baby was born with six fingers on each hand and six toes on each foot! They were shocked to see that when they weighed him, he weighed 16 pounds! He was unusually long, and they were astounded by the size of his "Tepulli" (Nahuatl language meaning penis)! It was so long that the Teopixque thought, "Surely he will sire many new Azteca!"

When they looked at his eyes, they were dismayed because it appeared as though his eyelids were transparent. This made him look as if he had more than two eyes. When his eyes opened, they appeared to be closed, and when they were closed, they looked as if they were open! The senior physician pointed this out to Chichinotpotl and then said, "My dear Emperor, I fear that as he grows, this child will have much difficulty with his sight. The sun will surely cause him pain and blindness, and if not, it will still be difficult for him to see clearly!" "Then we will give him an appropriate name; he will be called, "DIFICIL," (meaning difficult). As I look upon his eyes, my dear learned doctor, I must disagree with you. I believe that because of the condition of his eyes, this is a gift from the Gods! Look at how he is staring at me right now! Does it not seem that even though he was just born, he already sees?" Examining his eyes further, the Teopati realized that the emperor was right! The child seemed to already have good eyesight! The baby watched and reacted to every movement, and then he smiled! He smiled at everyone! The Emperor Chichinotpotl and the Empress were filled with jubilant pride as all the Teopixque and the Aguilas in the room went down to their knees in honor of this newborn "Pilli!"

There was brightness in the little boy's face as he wore a wide smile from ear to ear, and then he began blinking his right eye at his Nana! As she raised her head and saw him doing this, she laughed and was so happy to see that this newborn baby was so happy too! He was already playing games with her!

This is the story of a baby born to the royal family, the firstborn of Emperor Chichinotpotl and Empress Cuicani, of the Azteca nation in Tenochtitlan, (Mexico City, Mexico).

"One, two, three, four, five, six," the Empress was counting Dificil's toes and the fingers of his hands repeatedly! "So now tell me, my husband, with all your wisdom, what are these extra toes and fingers for?" Chichinopotl just smiled as he held one of his baby's little hands and said, "Right now, only the Gods know!"

Upon first learning of the pregnancy of the Empress, observations of the Sun, Moon, and stars were carried out by the Teopixque and the other soothsayers. It was said that the stars were aligned in a rare configuration similar only to one other time in the history of man, the birth of the Aztec God Quetzalcoatl. Such a statement prior to this time would have been viewed as blasphemy and heathenism of the lowest and vilest kind. But this was the time of the "La Primavera" (the springtime), and most importantly, the time in which the Aztecs believed to be the creation of the current world age, the "Fifth Sun," when their great empire flourished as did their Toltec ancestors before them!

This was a period of rebirth when the Gods smiled upon the earth. This was the time of the creation of ………DIFICIL!

Drums roared in syncopated rhythm; the Gods were celebrating in the heavens with the sound of thunder! Priests, noblemen, slaves and all the creatures of the earth were allowed to pass in review, bow, salute and bestow reverent prayers to the Gods and well wishes upon the newborn, the son of the ruler of all men.

Chapter Two
"A Celebrated Birth & A New Era"

Empress Cuicani laughed at her baby because as the drums roared their beat, Dificil moved his little toes in time with them! She thought it amusing also that when all the people passed in review, she saw the look of surprise and wonderment on their faces as Dificil smiled and fluttered his little eyes at them. All his eyes!

It was a glorious morning, as witnessed by all the servants who had prepared the beautiful and elaborate floral arrangements throughout the great capital city of Tenochtitlan. Never before were there so many nations' leaders present to honor the birth of a son, to pay homage to the future Tlatoani (Aztec emperor), the one who would decide their destiny.

Tasty food of every kind, of every animal and fowl born of this earth, was brought forth and presented as gifts to the newborn and his blessed family. The nation's people came from everywhere. They came from as far north as the snow country and all the way east and west from ocean ports, where there were huge creatures that swam in the sea known as "Pescadortoz" (whales). Chichinotpotl noticed how, at times, Dificil made seemingly painful grimaces and frowned at the sight of different people who passed by him. His father believed that Dificil was startled by quite a few who looked so grotesque and ugly!

Many people with their caravans brought frozen delicacies, rich in taste, cured and blessed. Other eastern kingdoms ruled by the Aztecs brought herbs and spices, planted and harvested from the soil, others from lofty trees and still other vegetarian delights preserved for the tasteful enjoyment of the anointed child and his family from the south. Other subservient nations brought rich gifts of gold, silver, emeralds and rubies. Fine rugs made from the pelts of exotic animals and soft, delicate bed coverings and sheets made from woven silk, which were said to be gifts from the Gods themselves, were presented to Dificil. What wonderment, what joy! It was evident that all the people were delirious with pride, love and happiness. They were numb with the realization that it would be written, that they would be part of this great history, marking the Day, the Year and the Place of the birth of the great Dificil!

Aside from his mother, he lay resting, wrapped in rich silk and cloth blankets interwoven with the bright sparkling gold hair from only the most powerful and healthy lions. She watched as Dificil rubbed his hands over the soft blankets and giggled and cooed at their touch. His bed of pure gold and silver railings with mosaic marble as its base was laden with bright, multi-colored feathers from exotic swans and Amazonian birds brought from the southern poles of the empire and cushioned with the soft skins of Black Bears, Brown Bears and the huge, snowy white Polar Bears of the north.

As with everything else about the birth of Dificil, the Teopixque were shocked to see that he was born with a full head of hair. The royal headpiece that had already been made for him was beautiful. It was the combination of huge eagle feathers, multi-colored heron feathers and quills from the wings of other exotic winged creatures. The headpiece had plumes that arched high above his head and were secured by gold talons. These were proudly and laboriously fitted together by the young "Aguilas" (Aztec Knights), who had fought in the tribal competition to win such an honor. The plumes were the color of green, of course, signifying the Jaguar, the elite symbolic banner of his lineage. As he looked up smiling, he continued his count, "One hundred eighty-three, hundred eighty-four."

No one heard or realized that Dificil was counting the feathers that adorned his father's headpiece. He was born at sunrise, about 4:00 o'clock in the morning today, and already he could count and sense danger and diagnose sickness and disease, a natural-born Teopati, a healer! He was also blessed with the gift of "Mental Telepathy."

He frowned as the oldest of his maid servants, his Senior NaNa, wiped his forehead, for she was close enough to him that he could feel her pulse, and he heard her labored breathing. He knew she did not have long to live because of a weak heart. As she looked at him, he could hear her saying soft words to soothe him, even though no words were spoken from her lips. It was through her mind that thoughts were communicated to him! On the other hand, when he was being held by his father, he smiled with happiness because he could tell how healthy he was. He felt his strength and vigor. Dificil gazed at the Aguilas and knew that it was about time for their relief, because a few hours after he was born, he noticed how they changed guards every hour, on the hour.

Each Aguila had the scent of complete cleanliness, as was the requirement of their position, and it meant death to those who did not adhere to this rule. Theirs' was a lifetime dream come true, a supreme honor, to be able to guard "Dificil" the heir of the Aztecas, the one who would be the ruler of the nation. Dificil was pleased and awed at the dazzling colors worn by each Knight. Their military apparel had been handmade. Countless hours it took the most skilled seamstresses to create such beautiful soldiers' ware. Each piece of their uniforms was intricately interwoven with silk, cotton and gold lace. Their hair was clean and slightly oiled to allow for neatness and was tightly kept in a pearl-laden cross tie. Multi-colored eagle feathers worn atop their heads depicted their position of honor, their imperial duty and their military ranking. They were fully trained and skilled in all forms of "Tlahtlacolli" (Nahuatl language meaning military preparedness), supremely physically fit, experts in a vast array of fighting techniques/Martial Arts, use of weaponry, emergency first aid, navigational techniques and other disciplines. One of their most important training exercises was the art of "Ando Ciego," known as the "Blind Walk."

It was the ability to travel through thick brush, woods, and mountain ranges in complete darkness. These men and a few choice women could go without food or water for extreme lengths of time and could survive any terrain, any weather and extreme pain. Rarely was there an enemy who would be so foolish as to challenge such elite, fierce warriors!

With great delight and such a huge smile on her face, the
senior Nana began to address the Empress Cuicani, "Oh dear
Empress, your son continues to feed himself without end. He has
already fed from your breast, mine, four of the other Nanas
(Nannies), and now he is suckling on the breast of his aunts!"
Everyone was amazed because even though he was born just
eight hours ago, they felt sharp scrapes from his teeth from his
suckling of the natural milk! Now night was upon this serene
city. The clear sky was the color of orange on the horizon, the
sun and moon met and smiled upon the great Aztec Prince!

As the days, hours and weeks slowly went by, Dificil was
growing anxious. Finally, the time arrived when he was ready,
more than willing and able to venture outdoors! While everyone
but his royal guard slept, Dificil quietly crawled to a corner of
his blanket covering and jumped to the marble floor. Then, in the
dark, he softly crept to a doorway and slipped by the guards out
into the open, still air. "Ah, this is wonderful," he exclaimed as
his little feet carried him to the edge of the woods. The stars
shone bright, the birds were suddenly quiet and still, all the
animals paused, for Dificil joined them in the forest, and they
were at peace with his presence! Sometimes he walked,
sometimes he ran and at times he seemed to float through the
brush. His movements were smooth, easy, silent and quick. As
birds flew above him, the other animals followed close by and
guarded his flank, his rear and cleared the way in front of him.

Dificil leapt like a panther and, with the strength of a jaguar,
ran with powerful strides alongside the deer and antelope, and
like all of the animals, he could see in the night as if it were day.
Playing with the many different animals as he moved further on

into the thick woods, he laughed and shrieked with sheer excitement and love for his fellow creatures of the earth.

"Nilze, Nilze, nocenyeliz. Ni pactia tlachia, Ni pactia tlahoa Ni nehnemi mitz," (Nahuatl language meaning), "Hello! Hello, my family. I am so happy to see you, to talk to you and walk with you," he exclaimed to his animal friends. He and they knew they were as one. They could feel his love, and he could feel theirs' and together they were enjoying life, the fresh air and a time of peace. Dificil easily climbed tall trees as he jumped from one branch to another, finally resting upon the tallest of all the oaks and looked out upon his kingdom, his world and his sleeping people. As all his animal friends watched, Dificil gauged his surroundings, north from south, east from west, and he counted the stars. He awed at the brightness of the North Star, and he smiled as he recognized the configurations of all the heavenly designs. Some he knew were recorded in the holy books of the Teopixque, and others would not be discovered for centuries to come! "Look there, the "Big Dipper," "Leo the Lion," and "Pluto."

"Oh! Oh! Where did the time go? I must be getting back before someone notices I'm missing," Dificil screamed out as he began to run back towards the palace. He giggled as it amazed him how he was able to slip out into the night, unnoticed, but not alone or unguarded, for he was accompanied and protected by his animal friends. Dificil knew he must return to his family's royal temple before anyone discovered he was gone. Surely his Aguilas would be put to death because it would appear they had failed in not being alert enough to prevent his departure alone and away from their protection and his majestic palace, his home!

Chapter Three
"Midnight Adventure"

Upon returning to the palace, Dificil was already planning the forthcoming evening. He was excited, for he knew that he would again sneak out into the country and speak and play with his many friends. As the moon settled high in the sky, at the stroke of midnight, Dificil was already in the woods. This was only his second time venturing into the forest. His feet barely touched the brush as he swiftly ran with delight! Suddenly, he stopped. He saw two white eyes before they saw him. Gingerly, carefully and with a strange timidity, a young animal walked toward Dificil. The huge, animal covered in white fur stopped right in front of Dificil and moaned at his feet. Dificil began speaking to the large animal, "Do not fear, my dear friend, I will not hurt you! Come closer that I may place my hand upon your head and pet your soft fur." Moving forward and sitting just at the feet of Dificil, the young timber wolf slowly licked Dificil's hand and cooed as he now relaxed. "Come, follow me and let us enjoy this wonderful evening together. We will run through the woods. We will swim in the creek, and we will enjoy the company of all the rest of our friends here in the forest," Dificil joyfully exclaimed. The timber wolf did not know that Dificil had heard him many times before as he howled at the moon in the still of the night. He no longer felt alone, even though he had separated himself long ago from his wolf pack. He somehow felt welcome and secure in the presence of Dificil. Dificil looked at the timber wolf with loving eyes, all his eyes and then said, "When I return home tonight, you will accompany me. I want you to stay with me from now on. I shall call you 'Llore,' (Nahuatl language meaning "to cry"), one who cries in the night and howls from deep within his heart!"

Dificil stopped at the base of a tall apple tree as a young monkey sitting atop one of the longer branches threw down one of the bright red apples and struck him in the head. The little monkey screamed with glee as all the other animals froze in fear and anticipation! "Why, you little rascal, I'll catch up to you and make you swallow that apple whole," Dificil declared. He laughed so hard it made his stomach ache as all the others nervously began to laugh too. Just then, as the monkey was leisurely hanging from another limb, he turned around and screamed! To his surprise, out of nowhere, Dificil was now sitting right behind him on the same limb! Dificil roared again with laughter as he held out his hand to the monkey. The monkey bowed to Dificil, lowering his head. As he had done to Llore, Dificil ran his hand over his soft fur and said, "I love you, my little friend. Come, follow us, and join us in more fun and adventure. Dificil and his many friends continued on through the thick forest. All the animals watched as he climbed one tree after another and leapt down to the ground, and then they all began running again. They ran around in circles."

They raced each other over and over again, all the time laughing and enjoying themselves. Finally, upon reaching a clearing in the woods, Dificil grew tired and stopped to rest by a beautiful little creek. The water was so clear and bright blue in color. Dificil sat down in front of a huge oak with his feet in the water and began to catch his breath and rest his little legs. He hummed a happy tune as all the many birds surrounding him sang along in unison. This seemed to be such a quiet, serene place. The young monkey brought him some fresh berries and nuts from the trees nearby. Dificil happily ate the fruit and nuts as beautiful, multi-colored butterflies sat atop his shoulders, much to the wonderment of Llore, who now stood guard next to him.

As Dificil continued to sit and rest, he began to reflect on his world, his family, and his people. In his mind, he began to review all his studies and lessons. With each day's passing, Dificil learned so many things quickly. His mind absorbed and retained as if it were a sponge. All seven of his senses were in constant operation and alert! Upon first meeting someone, Dificil could detect whether their spirit was good or evil.

Along with his ability to see from long distances, he could see through the darkness at night, and he could hear from a great distance as well; thus, his hearing and sight were as keen as his animal friends. He utilized his gift of mental telepathy to communicate with his senior NaNa as well as with his animal friends. Dificil could also communicate through his sense of feeling and body motions, just like the animals; body language was used as another form of communication. The animals were so much more appreciative of the land, the stars in the skies, the four winds, the sun and the moon. Shadows left messages, mirages revealed vivid signs, and touch, smell and sound reminded you that you were alive!

As Dificil reflected over the many conversations he had heard from his people over the past few months, it troubled him that so many had such backward, negative thoughts. He wondered aloud, "Why must people make things so complicated? Can they not see the plain view in front of them? They don't even take enough time to remember that there are fingers at the end of their hands and toes at the end of their feet! They are so busy complaining about what they think they haven't had in the past, to bother to take time out and realize and enjoy what they have in the present! Together, my father, my mother and my Teopixque friends need to speak with our people and awaken them as to their many gifts. We must remind them not to take for granted what we have now, for soon in the near future, much of that will be lost forever," Dificil sighed. "Oh well, come Llore, it is late, and we must hurry and return to the palace before someone finds out we are gone," Dificil called out to his new huge, furry friend.

Once again, Dificil began to run as all his friends followed him to the end of the forest and bid him goodbye. He and Llore silently entered the door of the palace, returning to Dificil's bed chamber. Llore now took his place at the foot of Dificil's bed and stood guard as his young master laid down to rest. The first light of this new morn was only about an hour away, and there was a smile upon Dificil's face as he peacefully drifted into a deep slumber, remembering when he was born!

Chapter Four
"A New Day"

Only a few years had passed, and everyone was amazed at the speed of Dificil's growth. He not only grew in size but also in his ability to function already as a full-grown adult. All the Teopixque, awed at his uncanny ability to absorb their lessons so easily. These were the teachings of their religion and prayers, identifying and naming deities and military ranks, the beginnings of math, engineering, astronomy, and his basic royal duties. Very few people had seen him since his birth and did not know anything about his miraculous intellectual and physical advances.

As usual, at night, he didn't sleep long, but it was enough to refresh him. He usually woke up before sunlight each day. There were the sounds of conch horns, flutes, bells, and drums. Dificil could hear the coordinated cadence of the Aguilas' feet. They marched and ran in unison to their stations and at times, grunted and sang a variety of songs as they drilled together. He noticed how everything was done so formally and so practiced. These Aguilas were trained with so much precision and discipline, and they worked as one. As Dificil peered outside the palace door, he suddenly noticed a strange, foul odor! What was that smell? It seemed as though maybe an animal had gotten sick and died with its flesh rotting in the hot sun! His sense of evil, danger and desolation was astonishing and unwavering. He knew something was desperately wrong, but he didn't want to face it right now. He was still so young and inexperienced, but his instincts did not lie! He needed for someone to tell him that this wasn't death that entered his sensitive nostrils. There must be some mistake, some terrible error!

Dificil jumped up and ran past the senior Aguila at the entrance door of the palace. The Aguila grimaced and screamed out an alarm. Immediately, the royal guard sprang into action and ran after little Dificil as he scurried towards the center of Tenochtitlan. The bodyguards could not believe their eyes! How could this little child run so fast, "By the Gods," with the speed of a gazelle! Why was he running to the pyramids and away from the safety of his palace? The guards could not keep up with him and were only able to keep sight of him as he quickly ascended the steep steps of the Great Pyramid of Sacrifices, the main pyramid of Tenochtitlan, Tlaloc.

What had just begun as a bright sunny sky, now suddenly turned dark, filled with huge forbidding clouds, and a strong wind picked up as lightning struck and loud thunder roared! The earth shook and all went down to their knees, for they felt a great fear. They sensed a catastrophic happening, a rebuke from the Gods! Dificil reached the top of the pyramid and yelled as loud as his little lungs could yell, "Stop, drop your knives and your evil swords. There will be no more executions, no more sacrifices today!" As Dificil spoke, his voice reverberated so loud and distinct. It was as if his words came from the heavens and were echoed with the thunder! His little voice carried down upon his subjects. It traveled across the waters and into the plains and continued through the great Sierra Madre Mountains. As the

Aguilas looked up to the top of the pyramid, Dificil could be seen, and a trembling fear gripped them because they could not help but see the ominous look of Dificil's piercing eyes, all his eyes! The Teopixque dropped to their knees in horror. They wailed in fear, and their hands dropped the obsidian blades. Bodies were strewn all around Dificil. Almost on every step were the remains of unfortunate souls who had been defeated as enemies of the Azteca warriors and surrendered, only to be brought forth before the sacred altar to be sacrificed. The steps of the Great Pyramid had turned scarlet red with the blood of the vanquished enemies! Dificil's bodyguards came to a stop in front of him, dropping to their knees and bowing their heads in reverence to the young prince, filled with the grave, unmistakable sense of danger!

Upon being summoned, his father, the great Chichinotpotl, quickly climbed the steep steps of the pyramid and called out to his son, "Dificil, my son, what is wrong? Why do you weep, and how is it that you have turned a bright, peaceful day into a horrific, dark, stormy night?" Dificil's father was followed by his wife, the Empress Cuicani. She too dropped to her knees and called out to Chichinotpotl, "My dear husband, I humbly warn you, take heed of the prophetic words of our son. Can you not feel his power, his strength and his awesome control right now of everything that is life?" Dificil's father lowered his head not in fear, but in awe and trembling respect as he yelled out, "What manner of human has my wife borne into this world? How is it that even the clouds seem to move upon Dificil's command, and his stare surely could melt the spirit of the most courageous warrior?"

Dificil looked up to the sky with his little hands raised above him. With his tear-filled eyes, he seemed to be praying. Then, as he again looked down upon the steps of the great pyramid, he gasped at the sight of hundreds of torn bodies lying on each step. Why some of their hearts still beat even though they had been carved out of their bodies by the Teopixque and laid upon the altar! There were no other sounds but the wind, the rain, and the thunder of Dificil's voice. "Let it be known and let it be written that no Azteca shall kill another human being to be set forth as a sacrifice! Whoever does not fear the gates of hell, the 'Underworld,' then let him come before me now and chance his life, his families' future, his own being! I speak not on my own but as a messenger of things to come!"

As the bodies were carried away and the other prisoners that were still alive were taken back to their cells, the sky suddenly released a soft sun shower. The rain poured, and the blood was washed away from the steps of the great pyramid. A magnificent, wonderful rainbow appeared, and once again, the music of the birds could be heard, and there was peace all around! The Teopixque stared in disbelief and stood with their heads bowed before Dificil. This child is surely the "One!" The "Pilli," (Prince) of foretold lore, here, in real life, a miraculous being! Dificil's father called him, and he slowly descended the steps of the pyramid. As his father watched, Dificil raised his right hand and touched the head of each Teopixque and Azteca warrior he passed. Upon reaching his parents, Dificil was just like any other child. He was smiling and seemed once again to be happy as he reached out and took his father's hand. "Yes, this is my baby, my precious Dificil," the Empress Cuicani proudly exclaimed as she put her arms around Dificil and hugged him tight.

Though her eyes were still filled with tears, she was happy with the knowledge that her Dificil was safe and well. Expressing relief, she hugged him so tight that Dificil blurted out, "Mommy, stop, you squeeze me so hard that I can't breathe." Hearing this Chichinotpotl laughed out loud, realizing that this great being was still his son, his little boy. There was a warm glow about him. His very presence commanded awe and respect, and his essence seemed to echo peace, love, and the serene feeling of tranquility.

From atop the pyramid, at the moment he had given the command for all the Teopixque to stop killing, Dificil had saved one special vanquished enemy, a warrior chieftain who was from a southern "Calpolli" (tribe), the Maya. Unbeknownst to anyone, he was a "Pilli" like Dificil, a royal, a prince, and one day he would repay this act of mercy, this kindness from Dificil and come to his rescue and help save the Aztec nation!

Chapter Five
"Meeting & Greeting"

Occasionally, some mornings after "Tenia," (Nahuatl language meaning, breakfast), Dificil would go, accompanied by his bodyguards and the rest of his entourage to the marketplace located in the center of Tenochtitlan. Here he had the opportunity to see the many different people, "Calpolli" (tribes) that traveled to this great city to trade and buy goods. His bodyguards were astounded each time because they could hear Dificil immediately speaking to each one in their own language. Somehow, the young prince could instantly adapt, understand and speak the stranger's native tongue. Dificil was always very courteous and genuinely friendly when he talked to anyone. He did not mind the people who stared as they watched his every move after first bowing and lowering their heads when he was right in front of them, because no one was supposed to look directly at him. Once he walked passed them, they were able to look at him, and they were awed by the strange look of his eyes. They wondered, "How could he see when it appeared his eyes were closed, or were they open? Should he not be blinded by the sun because his eyelids seemed to be transparent? Why were his eyes not filled with dust from the winds and moisture from the rain?" Dificil seemed to read their thoughts, and he could not help but smile and laugh at their lack of knowledge; they seemed to be so naïve. This thinking of his was not in arrogance or feelings of superiority but in wonderment that they too, were not as gifted as he.

Dificil spoke just as polite to the "Macehuales" (the free common folk), as he did to the many "Pipiltin," (nobles). This interaction with the Macehuales was very wise, because they were from Calpultin (tribal clans). They were, according to ancient custom, as farmers, assigned their own place where the agricultural "Chinampas," (floating gardens) were developed within the four-quarter plot of the capitol city of Tenochtitlan, thus their importance because they cultivated the crops and paid tribute for their farming privileges to the nobility. This bothered some of the Teopixque because they felt that Dificil should not even converse with the lower class. They thought that it was beneath him to talk to them. Although they disliked this open communication Dificil practiced, they dared not interfere or try to correct him, for he was the baby king, the great Emperor Chichinotpotl's heir.

One day, Dificil noticed a lady with six children waiting in line to buy tortillas of "Maize" (corn flat dough). Dificil could not help but notice that her clothes and her children's clothes were so ragged, and they all looked as if they were starving. It saddened him very much to see this woman and her children in such a condition. He walked up to her as she and everyone in line immediately dropped to their knees.

Dificil took her by the arm and said, "Please rise, dear mother, I wish to speak to you." Still frightened, the frail woman rose with her head bowed as she began to speak, "I am just a poor woman who is trying to feed her children. I am not worthy to speak to you, my dear lord." "Why is it that your husband does not accompany you here and assist you with your duties?" asked Dificil. "Oh, great one, my husband has been dead for at least a year. He was killed in a battle defending one of your outside provinces," she replied. Then Dificil asked, "As an Aguila's widow, why were you and your children not cared for as is the usual procedure within the royal Aguila order, especially since your husband died protecting our empire?"

"My husband was a bearer of military banners and, as such, was not yet an Aguila when he was killed in battle. Please do not trouble yourself, for I am just a lowly widow," she concluded. Dificil could not believe what he just heard! He could not understand how a warrior protecting his kingdom did not deserve to have his wife and family looked after. Just then, one of the Teopixque, believing that the woman was bothering Dificil with begging for food, began to push her and her children away. Dificil turned towards him, enraged, and yelled at him, "Take your hands from that woman and her poor children, do you not see her suffering already?" At that moment, one of the Aguila bodyguards raised his ax to strike down the Teopixque, thinking that he had touched or offended Dificil in some way. Dificil stopped the Aguila from killing the elderly Teopixque. "No, do not strike him, I want him just to leave my presence and return to the temple. I don't think he meant to annoy me or cause me any displeasure. Dear Teopixque, you need to go and fast and pray for forgiveness for being so cold and with such little compassion for such a poor soul," he said, rebuking the old priest. While this was going on, the hundreds of people who were all around stopped all activity and became silent as they listened to this exchange between Dificil, the widow, and the old Teopixque. Everyone around was astounded at such a kindly gesture by the great Pilli! To think that the royal heir to the Azteca throne would even bother to care about the condition of a poor widow!

Just then, one of Dificil's most senior Teopixque asked to speak to him. After the incident with the widow, the elder Teopixque stepped forward and knelt down in front of Dificil. Responding to the old priest, Dificil said, "My dear teacher, of course you may speak to me. As always, I honor and appreciate your presence and your good counsel." The Teopixque began by saying, "First, I would ask that you allow me to personally arrange for this poor widow and her children to be escorted to one of our temples so that our servants can provide them with food and a chance to freshen themselves. May I also say that your kindness warms my heart and, as always, endears you to all those around you. They hear and witness your goodwill and your wisdom in relating to your people." Answering him, Dificil said, "I thank you, and yes, I would appreciate it that you arrange for the caring of this mother and her children. I also want you to set up provisions and a permanent home for her here in Tenochtitlan, so that she may be close and I can keep track of her and personally see to her family's welfare. I want you to find out where her husband is buried and have his remains brought here so that we can provide a proper military funeral with honors for him. I'm sure that would help console this poor widow and comfort her."

The Teopixque then bowed again and said, "I will see to it that your directions are followed exactly as to the care and comfort of this widow and her children. I humbly advise you to be alert and careful because what enemies we may have, may take your kindness as a sign of weakness," advised the Teoppixque. Dificil shook his head, reflecting on what the priest had just warned him about and said, "It is most unfortunate that somehow we must always take heed as to our actions and our social activities because of potential threats from those around us! Your words are wise and true, my dear Teopixque, but know this, that any fool that would mistakenly take my kindness and generosity as a weakness or vulnerability would find out very quickly that such an assessment would be a fatal mistake! I do not take kindly to anyone who would wish to use my compassion as an opportunity to criticize or worse, to attack me or my family, my people! Yes, please proceed with our plans and do not worry about anything else," exclaimed Dificil.

After hearing Dificil's response, the Teopixque shook from fear with the realization again that Dificil was far advanced in his perceptions of people and that he was too wise to be taken advantage of. This as always, amazed all the Teopixque and at the same time filled him with admiration for the young Pilli because he saw through Dificil's words, his instant response, that he would be a very dangerous person, and a deadliest adversary to go against! Dificil turned his attention back to the widow and told her to raise her head so he could see her face and look into her eyes. This amazed the Aguilas because of the standing decree that no one was supposed to look directly at Dificil. Dificil placed his hand under the woman's chin and lifted her head. He saw the tears in her eyes and such a look of fear and desperation! Instantly, the poor widow began to openly weep. She still felt that she must be dreaming a wonderful dream because how was it possible that a great man, a Pipiltin such as Dificil, would bother to concern himself with the welfare of her and her children! Dificil reached down and picked up the bag the widow had placed on the ground and handed it to one of the Teopixque. He took her hand and told her, "Please dear woman, go now with the Teopixque so that they may escort you to the palace and care for you. You need not worry anymore, and I would pray that you will soon find comfort and rest." As she was led away by the Teopixque and Aguilas, the surrounding crowd opened a path through which she walked towards the temple. As she left, the huge crowd dropped again to their knees and shouted out, "Dificil! "Teotl! Dificil! Teotl" – (Nahuatl language meaning Wonderful Dificil, A God, Wonderful Dificil, A God!"

Chapter Six
The Protector, "Little Feather"

"Perhaps Little Feather, you will learn to be more patient and acquire additional skills instead of becoming more stubborn and keep shaking your tail and your little head no," his blind father said. This was not just an admonishment but another lesson for his gifted son to absorb. "You will meet your friend soon enough. You must continue to study, learn, prepare, be alert and ready for your meeting with him," exclaimed his father, El Vision (The Vision). "But father, why must I continue to study so much each day? The sun, the moon, the stars, the cumulus clouds and the foretelling of the rains, all complicated lessons that I'd rather not endure," asked his loveable, impatient son.

"Ahi, my little boy, those subjects are just a touch of your studies, will you discard and forget the rest?" Do you not sense your true destiny, your extended power and knowledge?" We both understand and must reverently remember our life's purpose here on earth! Come Little Feather, open up your heart, unlock your mind and see all that most do not see, for your time is near and your true destiny is at hand!"

"El Vision" was a renowned elder. No one knew how old he was. Some said he was around from the beginning of time, a blind man who spent his days tending to his many plants, flowers and herbs before their traveling began. He spent most of his time with Little Feather, his five-year-old son. He watched over him as he slept, he prepared his special meals, and he taught him all the wonders of the world in preparation for his foretold meeting, his mission, with the great "Dificil!"

The old gentleman was said to be blind only because his eyes did not see. He carried a staff which he used avidly not only to assist him in his daily sojourns with Little Feather, but also to illustrate in the dirt and sand the lessons he provided for him. Little Feather marveled at the sight of a light at the top point of his staff that would help guide their way at night. Most of the time a huge, beautiful bald eagle flew just above them, its bright, sharp eyes focused on all their surroundings. It was said that the eagle regularly spoke to El Vision, advising him on his plotted trails and guiding him on his path and as such, was given the name "Itta" (meaning "to see").

El Vision hiked through the mountainous regions of southern and northern Mexico. Accompanied by Little Feather, he showed him the many trails and pathways they could walk, where not even a mountain goat could travel. They could climb where there seemed to be no crevice to hold onto, nor a pocket in the stone to grip. He taught him about all the natural resources that were afoot and in the trees. He showed him a vast array of plant life that grew within the crevices of the mountain and the most edible greens, herbs, fungi and seeds, unknown to most men. He taught him that with a true union, respect and understanding of the plants and all animal life, man could learn much in his quest not only to survive, but to grow and prosper.

Through these travels, Little Feather learned of the white stuff that fell from the sky, which they called "Nieve" (snow). He was taught through the many demonstrations by his father and their animal friends how one could successfully search to find water. He learned how to obtain ice from the many cold mountain water pools and use it in preserving food and drink. In one instance, while in the desert, he watched as a rare creature, unknown to most men, called a horse, traversed in circles in the sand and, through its sense of smell, detected the right place to dig and find enough water not only to drink, but abundant enough to bathe in!

While traveling with his father, Little Feather was taught how to pick an object before him and use its shadow throughout the day to tell time. He learned through studying the clouds, the feel of the wind and the smell of the air how to forecast the weather, its changes and variations. He was taught not only to use the North Star as a guide for travel, but also the different constellations of stars, the flight of birds, the migration of herds of bison and sheep and the change in foliage and soil. These were happy times for the little one. He enjoyed the many hours and days he spent traveling with his father, experiencing the endless, beautiful landscape they called Earth. Even though El Vision was blind, Little Feather was awed at his dexterity, his agility and how sure footed his father was as they journeyed across the plains, atop the mountains, through the valleys and amongst the forest of trees. As they continued on their journey, Little Feather was fascinated as he met with different Calpolli (Tribes). He and his father stood long enough in each village, city and camp to grasp and understand their languages, cultures and customs. Every time they met with different people, it seemed as if everyone already knew his father, and they would immediately bow before both of them, demonstrating so much caring and respect. Little Feather noticed they all spoke of the Azteca in the same manner. The Azteca were revered by most of the "calpolli," hated by some and feared by all! While conversing with all the people, his father told everyone that this would be the first of a few opportunities they would have to see Little Feather, and they displayed pride and reverence upon this meeting. They seemed to know that he was a child of destiny and would somehow be responsible for their future.

"Could I touch his hand," one would ask. Another would seek to embrace him or place the palm of their hand upon his forehead for good fortune and protection from the evil spirits. Little Feather did not understand why all this focus and attention was on him, or why there was a look of solemn fear in the eyes of many who looked upon him. He thought deeply about this, knowing he would have to ask his father what this all meant, as he and his father had just left the last village and continued on their arduous journey. As they crossed one of several waterways en route to Tenochtitlan Little Feather asked, "I'm nobody special, what do they imagine is different from me to them," as his feet were suddenly webbed and he paddled in the clear water, and there appeared a large slit on each side of his head, like those of the gills of a fish.

Swimming with powerful strokes and great speed, they made it quickly across the river! Upon reaching the shore, he and his father ascended a hill, and suddenly Little Feather stepped forward with his little feet, which had rounded arches and twelve toes, and then the openings on the side of his head once again disappeared! "Father, you must tell me of this place, Tenochtitlan, the imperial city, the home of the Azteca. I would like to know what I should expect to see when we get there. I would like to know how people will look and what language they might speak. Should I be afraid, or should I be comfortable with whom I meet? Will they be warm and friendly right away or will they be arrogant and cold," asked Little Feather. Now, Little Feather, why would you think anything negative about your initial meeting in Tenochtitlan? Stay focused and ready, for when you will meet with Dificil! As we enter the land of the Azteca, you will see for yourself the beauty and majesty of their kingdom. You will know immediately that you have been blessed to be part of the Pipiltin and feel the warmth and closeness of being part of the royal family and living in the magical city!

El Vision looked proudly upon his son, his little package of a prize. They stopped to make camp and cook "Tlacualli," food. As he started the fire, El Vision sensed their destiny, and with that destiny, he felt sadness with the knowledge that his time with his beloved son was short and near an end.

"Ahi! Little Feather, your questions are sometimes as numerous as the stars in the sky, but your queries are as intelligent as always." Little Feather just shook his head in wonderment, but smiled because he knew that everything his father said was true.

Through his daily lessons, his father always told him about the future and so many things to come. Little Feather realized that his father was preparing him for the future, his destiny and his foretold great task in life! How many children after him would know, or would be able to understand, that they had been set upon this blessed earth for such an important mission, fulfilling prophecy? Little Feather finally realized that he actually was quite different from all other children of his age. He was born with special gifts, and he was very powerful and strong. He would use everything he learned in the service of someone greater and more gifted than he, and it would be his lifelong responsibility to protect this person, for he was crucial to the future of the rest of their world and their destiny!

"Stay confident, my son, fear no one and wonder not of your safety for it is written that you shall hold a special place. You shall gain a lifelong friend, a brother, who will love and protect you, but who will also need your protection and advice. Now sleep, my son, and let the morrow answer all your questions and bring you to your rightful place in the sun," El Vision told Little Feather as he rocked him in his arms. With that, Little Feather closed his sleepy eyes and began to dream that he was riding a white horse with one silver horn upon its head, carrying him over a city of gold! El Vision covered him with a fine, multi-colored "Sarape" (blanket) and he too, contented and at peace, drifted off to sleep as all the nearby animals stood watch and guarded the coming of "Dificil's Shield!"

CHAPTER SEVEN
"REST & SURROUNDINGS"

It was a brisk morning, and Little Feather shivered as he awoke to the wonderful smell of "Tortillas de Maiz," (corn tortillas), venison meat and beans mixed with "chiles," (peppers). As always, El Vision prepared Little Feather's meals with all the nutrients, vitamins, iron and minerals he needed to keep him healthy and growing strong. Chiles were especially beneficial because they provided him with vitamins A and C. Often, El Vision would serve Little Feather "Huautli," Amaranth, for it was a very high-protein grain that was second only to maiz. Little Feather rubbed his sleepy eyes and smiled as he watched his father prepare their breakfast. The morning skies were clear with a deep blue color and bore no sign of clouds. There was not a scent hinting at rain, and the bright sun seemed to smile upon this young boy and his father. Camping on the mountain top for the night was both restful and peaceful for Little Feather. As he walked over to the mountain spring and washed in the clean, cold water, he felt the urge again to ask his father many questions about things he had on his mind. It never ceased to amaze El Vision the awesome intelligence and great memory his son had. This was more evidence of the gifts he inherited from his beloved Amazon mother who had died giving him birth.

"Father, I noticed that you have the fire surrounded by a 'Trecena,' (13 stones pertaining to the Aztec Codex Borbonicus and the 260-day Aztec Tonalpohualli calendar). I remember you telling me over and over about the 13 Lords of the Day," exclaimed Little Feather. Each day was associated with its' own deity. El Vision did this to pay homage to the deities and to (as he strongly believed), bring blessings upon his precious son, for El Vision was a professional Deviner, a specialist who made prognostications for newborn children to give advice for future endeavors. This was especially essential to the purpose and foretold mission of Little Feather.

"It is true, my son and I have meant each one to be of a good sign for your blessing and protection," answered El Vision. "Oh great gods, I think I remember…., let me see…, oh yes, there is the Monkey, the Dog, the Rabbit, and the Deer. See Papa, I recognize the signs you have made," Little Feather proudly recited to his father. As he thought more of the signs and markings, he said, "I wonder what omens Papa has derived from the burning of the fire throughout the night? Oh my mind is tired already and I just woke up! It is fun to talk to my father from afar, even though I cannot hear what he says, but can read his lips, and I still wonder how we can also communicate through our minds!"

"Come, Little Feather, so you may eat and replenish yourself, for I'm sure you'll use a lot of energy with all your questions and you'll need your strength for what mischief you might get into later," he laughed. Little Feather noticed how the eagle, "Itta," kept looking at him, and he thought, "Itta is staring at me, and I wonder what he is thinking or trying to say. He began to concentrate hard, and then he said, "Let me see, I know! Yes, my dear friend. It is true. The earth is beautiful, and the air is so clean, and the sky is heaven! Yes, I do appreciate my surroundings. Why I was just watching how the water flows down the mountain and how such a waterfall seems so strong and powerful!"

"Yes, Little Feather, and I bet if you dove into the eye of the rushing waters, you could swim faster and stronger than the salmon who swim south on their yearly sojourn," answered the eagle.

Little Feather and his father had been traveling for many months. They had toured many, many pueblos and villages throughout the land. Now he seemed tired but very anxious to finally meet his predestined companion, his new brother! As the many days went by and he met many different Calpolli, Little Feather felt he was now ready and prepared enough to meet the great Pilli!

Every day, Little Feather woke up at the break of dawn and continued his studies and practiced his different disciplines. This morning, he sat still, he heard a strange, different sound. "I hear distant drums! I could feel them as if they were at my feet! I hear the blaring of conch horns blowing in the wind! I hear people chanting! What is it that they are chanting? Somehow I know! I recognize the sound! It is such a beautiful sound, so pleasant to the ears, and it makes my body vibrate as it echoes throughout the land. What is happening?"

All the birds had stopped chirping, and they were all perched upon the trees in silence. All the animals were still. The clouds had opened up and disappeared, showing clear, blue skies. The sun was now shining so bright and seemed to be focused upon an area just ahead, in front of where Little Feather stood, just north beyond the trees, across the waters of a causeway down into the area in front of the mountains! That sound, the name again! I know the name! Dificil! Dificil! Dificil! That's it! I'm coming, I hear you! Oh praises, blessings and glory! Yes, it's me, Little Feather! I'm coming, I'll be right there. I can hear you, and now I can see you! Please wait, my Lord! I will be there as fast as I can! Little Feather's feet suddenly diminished in size, they shortened in length, and they became hooves galloping into a blur. He rushed to his foretold partner, his dreamed of ruler and his friend!

El Vision felt and heard his son's steps disappear into the woods, running as fast as a rabbit, quicker than a cheetah, and as graceful as a deer! As he and the great eagle Itta followed his son's trail, a deep sadness overcame him. Once again, El Vision realized that his time with his son was near its' end as the dreams of so many years before had revealed to him. This was his quest. This was his purpose and the finality of his mission!

The sounds of the drums and music grew louder, and Little Feather's excitement was at a fever pitch as he got closer to the Great Dificil! As he exited the forest, his feet now changed into webbed fins, and once again, large slits opened on each side of his head. He continued with great speed to swim in the waters of the causeway. Now more than ever, he realized and appreciated all the lessons and training he had received from his father. He now understood clearly the importance, the necessity and the preparedness the lessons provided for him. He was ready, willing and able to come into the service of his friend, his lord and master, Dificil! History was being made. The glorious life of Dificil, his time to walk upon the earth and to reign over these great peoples had come to pass! Little Feather was finally meeting and uniting with him and the new era, the time of the "Fifth Sun" was upon the earth, and the skies echoed the glory of it all!

CHAPTER EIGHT
"THE 'PILLI' DIFICIL & THE TEOPIXQUE"

On this day, Dificil rose earlier than usual. He was so excited because his father had told him the night before that this would be a special day, a day when he would meet some of the other Teopixque, his teachers within the holy temple. He also told him he must leave Llore, his giant wolf at the palace, because this was the main place of worship. Dificil immediately instructed Llore of the same through their mental telepathy, and an involuntary moan escaped Llore's mouth! Since first becoming Dificil's canine companion, he had never once left his side. Nonetheless, even though he did not understand why this was necessary, he would follow his master's orders, but he would, of course, be anxiously waiting just outside of the temple for him.

Conch horns blared and drums could be heard loud and at a staccato beat at the announcement of the arrival of the great emperor Chichinotpotl and his son, the "Pilli," (the royal son) Dificil at the holy temple. As the huge doors to the sacred chambers were opened, there was complete silence inside as all the "Teopixque" (priest) were lined up down on their knees with heads bowed in welcome to the great Emperor and the prince of Tenochtitlan! As they entered the inner chamber of the temple,

Dificil felt chills flow through his body as he looked upon the "Holy Place" that was adorned with beautiful, elaborate sculptures and paintings that depicted different animals. A huge stone sculpture known as the "Stone of the Five Suns," (The Aztec Calendar) was placed at the foyer hallway entrance. The "Five Suns" indicated the creation and beginning history of the Azteca people. As he continued on into the temple, Dificil saw many Teopixque. There was a group of Teopixque for every God, and each one was clothed in long robes with hoods upon their heads, while still others could be seen who wore their hair very long. Some of the priests' hair was so long it reached down to their ankles. Some wore bright red robes with gold stitching and sparkling gold bracelets upon their wrist and ankles. Each wore a headdress, depicting his holy order and rank. Other priests wore gold loincloths and carried reed baskets filled with flowers and incense. After the arrival of the royal entourage, Chichinotpotl bid the Teopixque to continue on with their holy duties. Groups of Teopixque knelt in front of certain sculptures of deities and chanted. Still others were now going around the entire temple stepping in formation and striding in fixed movements to the sound of flutes, drums and reed instruments. As Dificil and his father proceeded to walk through the temple, Dificil suddenly stopped. In front of him was a Teopixque on his knees who had frozen as he observed the entrance of Dificil. Dificil instantly knew this Teopixque was different from the rest. As he looked upon him, he noticed that he was totally covered in some sort of earthen substance. Looking closer, Dificil could tell that the brown substance was soil. His finger nails were very long and curled, and his feet were covered in orange colored, reed-like moccasins. Dificil instinctively leaned forward and placed his right hand on the shoulder of the Teopixque and told him to rise. As he obeyed and rose to his feet, he still kept his head down in reverence to the emperor and Dificil. "Aha! I knew it was you! What my eyes did not immediately see, my inner self revealed your presence to me right away," Dificil happily announced.

"As I told you some time ago, Dificil, the Tlamatini will be the main Teopixque responsible for your studies and lessons. He will assist and train you and prepare you as the future Tlatoani of the Azteca Nation! He will be near you at all times and with his life, be responsible for your health and well-being," Chichinotpotl explained to his son.

The Tlamatini was described by all the Azteca as the "Wiseman," exemplary, a most important part of tradition, the leader of men, a companion, a bearer of responsibility, a guide. He was also a physician, a person of trust, a counselor, and an instructor. It was further said that, "He lights up the world, and he knows of the land of the dead!"

Upon the birth of Dificil, the Tlamatini was designated by Chichinotpotl to be the main one to personally see to Dificil's education and training and to advise Dificil as to all the social mores and traditions. Dificil sensed a warm feeling and a true trust of this learned Teopixque. Surprising everyone present, Dificil placed his arms around the Tlamatini and hugged him close to himself. When this happened, the Tlamatini moaned, involuntarily from fright. No one was ever allowed to be so familiar with "Pipiltin," (nobility). "Do not fear, my dear

Tlamatini. I am Dificil. You are my friend, my teacher and my companion. Dificil took his hand and then jumped back, exclaiming, "Your nails are really sharp!" I must be careful that you do not scratch me all the time! They are so sharp that I believe you could use them as weapons!" At that moment, his father sighed as he listened to his young son speak so irreverently to this Tlamatini inside the holy temple. This was not the first time that Dificil spoke so boldly to one of the Teopixque! "Dificil, my son, there is much you have yet to learn of the ways and means of these holy servants of the gods. I would ask that you be more careful in your manner of speaking and communicating with the Teopixque," Chichinotpotl instructed his son. "But Father, I only told him what is true. He does have sharp fingernails, and as I hugged him, dirt fell off of his body! I told him that I have never seen anyone like him before. I guess I still need more time to get used to the way they dress and all the other strange things about them," Dificil answered his father. Chichinotpotl just looked at his son and rolled his eyes, and held himself back from laughing out loud. He surely was so young and, as such, did not yet understand the formalities and customs applicable.

The sun brightly shone over the holy residence. Suddenly, many birds flew atop the temple and stood quietly as if they were entranced somehow and awaited a signal. Dificil proudly continued to walk with his father through the main concourse and then quietly sat amongst the Teopixque. Again, just before he sat, they instantly dropped to their knees in reverence to him. At that moment, the Tlamatini was aside Dificil. Dificil placed a hand upon his shoulder and caused him once again to tremble and gasp! What manner of child is this that bears the colors and crests of the royal family? Why is he just a little child and yet already commands respect, adoration and awe! As Dificil removed his hand from the old teacher, the priest was again able to breathe normally and sighed in relief. Dificil began to say, "Hey, you seem to be of good health and mostly normal, are you not comfortable with my presence before you? Why must you all tremble so? Is there a cold wind that has passed through you that I could not feel? Rise and look into my eyes that I might know you and henceforth recognize you." Dificil commanded. "What are those dark markings on your forehead, Ahi! They look like they hurt! Who did that to you?" Slightly embarrassed, Dificil's father reminded him again that the Teopixque could not rise before him and look into his eyes or face certain death. He went on to explain that the markings and colors all symbolized the level of importance and holy patronage of each Teopixque. Chichinotpotl further explained to Dificil the importance and meaning of this most holy place and that these Teopixque were picked for their particular worship of deities. Dificil began to cough from the abundance of incense that surrounded him and pushed open a small doorway to obtain some fresh air. All the Teopixque gasped at that moment and were so startled that some began to soil themselves from shock and fear. "Dificil, you must not open and close anything in this temple just because you feel like it! The doors, the windows, all the entrances and exit ways are specially designed for proper and ceremonial passage only," explained his father. As if he had not heard a word, Dificil was gathering up water in his hands from one of the huge pools of water and playfully splashed the Teopixque that knelt all around him. He laughed aloud and ran around the concourse singing and patted each one on his shoulder as he passed them.

"Dificil, you must stop such playfulness, this is not the proper time or place for such games and laughter," exclaimed Chichinotpotl. Let me see! Po-o-o-o-o-f! Yes, I can slide with ease. It seems so easy to glide across the temple floor! Look at the beautiful fish, so many different kinds and colors! O-o-oh! That water is so cold! That huge tank goes all around this floor! "Oh! How do they get the water to stay so clean and clear? What is that making bubbles? Such a long tube bubbling up into the water! Oh look at all the big bubbles!" Dificil screamed. As with many other great creations and inventions in Tenochtitlan, the Aztecas had developed a "water purification and filtration system." This is what Dificil called the "Bubble Maker." Chichinotpotl's eyes looked like they would pop out of his head as he called out to his son, "Dificil, Dificil!! You must stop your play. You must bring an end to such careless annoyance and disrespect for this holy place! Please, Dificil stop running and sliding back and forth across the great "Walkway!" (This was the floor that the Teopixque would walk on over and over as they chanted prayers and worshiped the deities). Oh Dificil! You can't put your hands in that water! No! No! Don't climb in there," his father yelled. It was too late! Much of the holy water splashed onto the shimmering floor and upon many of the Teopixque worshiping in their proper places around the "Walkway." Dificil seemed almost hysterical in laughter as he finally listened to his father and climbed out of the great pool. As some of the Aguilas hurriedly dried Dificil with soft cloths, he asked his father, "Papa, why do you worry? What is wrong? Is this not our place? Should I not enjoy my time here with these great wise men and share with them so much love, fun and laughter?"

"Dificil, you do not understand. This is a most holy place, a precious place of faith and prayer, a sanctuary, a meeting place of the Gods," exclaimed his father. "Papa, but I do understand more than you know! Why do you think I am so happy to be here amongst my friends? They too can play if they would like to! As you said Papa, this holy place is a sanctuary for not only us humans but the wonderful birds that are up their perched upon the pillars, the hundreds of multi-colored fish that I was swimming with and the many other creatures of the Great Spirit's that are here. I have peace and feel the presence of our ancestors here! Let me stay here father? I have much I would like to discuss with these Teopixque. I have many questions that I hope they can answer, and I suspect, as I help them relax and feel more comfortable, they will ask me many more!"

The great Chichinotpotl consented to his son's wishes and again was amazed how Dificil automatically made everything seem so simple, so easy, and so innocent. Hugging his father, Dificil walked towards the east end of the temple and gazed up at the great paintings, plants, trees and sculptures. Some of the trees inside the temple were huge palm trees with large orange, red, blue and pink birds and parrots perched upon them. He noticed the rubies, jade, marble and ivory that composed each square tile that he walked upon, and Dificil was filled with great pride at the artistry and craftsmanship of his people in creating and designing such beauty! As Dificil continued walking towards the huge golden "Podium of Teachings," many of the Teopixque rose from their knees and began to follow him. Gradually, the multitude followed each step of this young leader and began to hum a soft, low melody. The birds began to sing with them, and together their voices echoed the sounds of all the spirits past, emanating from the very walls of the temple. At that moment, all the Teopixque knew that this was such a profound happening and that a truly special, spiritual being was in their presence!'

Tears of joy flowed down the usually solemn faces of the Teopixque. A wave of euphoria swept over the gathering, filling everyone with a sense of accomplishment, bliss, and peace. They somehow knew that he came into their lives for a very special reason. "This is the "One," the Azteca Lord of prophesied teachings and long-awaited dreams!" All the Teopixque suddenly stood still as Dificil stopped at the foot of the "Podium of Teachings." He suddenly kicked off his moccasins as he stepped up to the podium and called out to the great wise men, "Come, do not fear, please join me, but don't slip on my moccasins! I have much to ask you! Will you not take time out to sit with me and enjoy this blessed opportunity to share the great history and glory of our people? Let me search your thoughts. Let me absorb your energy. Let us unite in our reverence and prayers. Let's join together on a sojourn of memories, folklore and dreams and talk of who we are and the prophecies of where we will be in the very near future!"

Once again, the great Teopixque were overwhelmed and trembled with wonderment as they listened to the words of the Great Dificil! They watched as always his eyes, all his eyes, appeared to be opened when they closed and closed as they opened, and together they began a most happy indulgence of themselves and their proud heritage. Dificil's face was all aglow, and it seemed as if the bright sunlight that shone from a skyline window above them, focused only on him. The Teopixque nervously gathered around him and sat and attentively began to listen to the "Little Emperor." One of the Teopixque did slip on Dificil's moccasins! Dificil reached down and helped him back up to his feet! The Teopixque stood in awe as they looked upon his refined features, reflecting his boyish looks that at the same time seemed to project a serious, peaceful creature. Such a being they had never before encountered in this world. His olive complexion seemed as smooth and perfect as new fallen snow. They noticed his hands were little and yet his twelve fingers were long and from his feet extended twelve toes, which were visible after he removed his moccasins.

Dificil began addressing the many Teopixque again, "I am honored to be here with you, my learned friends and teachers. Today, let us break bread together and join in study and conversations of our people, our culture and rich history. I will be your student. You will be my teachers, and together we will learn many things. This is a precious time that we have together and an opportunity for me as your student to acquire much knowledge and information concerning our religious rites and ceremonies, the sciences, our laws, medicine, mathematics, engineering and the ranks and strategies of our military." I will sit and listen, I will pay attention, and I will remember! "Those of you that I touched upon your shoulder must know that I meant you no harm, nor ill will or tribulation of any kind. Did you not feel the warmth from my hand, my spirit of love and caring? For now, I am with you and I am part of you and I wish to learn from your experience, Nocenyeliz, (my family)."

Glory to the "Great Spirit" for this is the time of "La Primavera," (springtime), a time of new birth, good health and fortuitous destiny. Ours is a gifted nation of people who have been blessed with many gifts of intelligence, military might and scientific innovations. Ours is a glorious race, descendants of the mighty Toltecs. We are the rulers of the world, and we must strive to maintain our way of life because there are others out there who are envious of our nation. Other calpolli want what we have and will do whatever they can to get it! Take, for example, our medicine. Others come to us in search of treatment for pain and healing. Our doctors perform intricate surgeries and cultivate and develop healing herbs and spices. We have accomplished making many agricultural improvements, and with that, new ways to feed not just our nation but many others. I have visited and have seen the splendid creation of the Chinampas fields. My father first told me of how our great city of Tenochtitlan was built on water, and I have traveled through the causeways observing the creation of our systems of irrigation, aqueducts, water purification, plumbing and the use of hydraulics and many other methods of engineering. Amongst our many discoveries, we have already utilized solar energy. For other people on this earth, it will take hundreds of years before they even begin to experiment with such a natural resource of power.

Both the old and young Teopixque, all the Teopixque, just stood there with their mouths wide open. They could not believe their ears listening to this "Telpochtli" (royal young boy), the heir to the Azteca throne. It was not just his words but the content of his speech. They were astounded by what Dificil had just told them! How could it be that he already knew so much and spoke so well? Truly, he is one special being, a blessing from the Gods! The subject matter of his thoughts and the foresight of his predictions were seemingly from another world! Dificil also felt great exhilaration and pride being in the company of such learned holy men. As he looked at their stunned faces, he understood their wonderment and fears. They were just beginning to know him, and he realized that now he would learn so much more, for he was surrounded by some of the finest minds of the world! Of course, because they were Azteca! He was Azteca, and this was the empire of the Fifth Sun!

What a wonderful day to be alive.

Chapter Nine
I Knew You Were Coming!

Just then, there was a great commotion outside the temple. The royal Aguilas surrounded Dificil and warned the Teopixque to back away from him? Outside Dificil joined his father and the rest of the entourage. What was all the rancor and excitement? As they stepped to the exit way of the Great Temple, Dificil heard all the noise, the voices, the yelling. He suddenly felt an oncoming presence, and he knew what was waiting for him. A huge crowd had gathered below the steps leading up to the Great Temple. All the bickering and bartering noise of the merchants in the nearby plaza had stopped. Suddenly, there was no sound of drums, nor the laughter of children playing. All was subdued and quiet!

Dificil noticed that Llore, out of nowhere, was now standing at his side, ready to pounce on anybody who came near him. Llore was acutely alert, sensing something in the wind and, through his strong olfactory, smelled the strangers coming near Dificil!

An Aguila general rushed toward Dificil and Chichinotpotl, but then suddenly stopped as he saw Llore about to attack him. Dificil signaled Llore to stand fast and relax. He submitted to Dificil's command but growled as he sat still. The young officer requested permission to speak to Chichinotpotl. With his body vividly shaking, he bowed before the emperor, who asked, "What is all this about? You must tell me now that we are not in danger or have some Teopixque forecast a storm, an earthquake or some other forthcoming disaster," yelled the Emperor.

"Oh my lord, I come to you with urgent news! I humbly beg your forgiveness for the interruption of your time of worship in the temple, but I was at a loss to assess this incident before us. I performed my usual duties of maintaining a perimeter of defense, readiness of assault and even preparation if necessary, for the evacuation of the royal family! But then this! This strange incident, this precarious state of affairs," exclaimed the young General.

"Speak up! What is it, Juaquin? Answer your emperor, or I will have your head and those of your whole family! Can it be that this confusion just shows me your incompetence? What treachery befalls me even as I am with my son, worshiping? You are in command, supposedly in control. Why are you not answering me?" yelled Chichinotpotl. The young commander's whole body continued to shake in horror and shame. Dificil felt compassion for the General. He noticed how he was sweating profusely as he was filled with profound fear and regret of having failed his lord and emperor. Dificil grabbed the commander's hand and helped him to his feet, and told him to join the other Aguilas ahead of them. "You need not worry! With my father's permission, I think it would be better if you just rejoined your men at the bottom of the pyramid." Chichinotpotl looked at Dificil as he dismissed the commander and somehow knew that everything was alright.

Dificil took his father's hand in his and said, "Come Papa, please join me as we will meet our new friends who await us at the foot of this pyramid. Do not blame the poor General. It is not his fault or that of anyone else. It is what it is and it is what is meant to be," explained Dificil. Escorted by the Aguilas, Dificil, the great Chichinotpotl, and all the Teopixque began to make their way down the steep steps of the holy pyramid. Chichinotpotl smiled because he saw how Dificil was holding on to Llore's tail too, as they descended the pyramid.

Dificil already knew what had happened. Young Azteca braves in training, along with the regular Aguila sentries, observed in the distance a young boy running through the forest towards them. They were able to see that he ran so fast that it looked as if his feet did not even touch the ground! They witnessed his great speed swimming through the waterways towards Tenochtitlan. They also noticed a strange elderly man following behind this young intruder. Though slow in movement, he appeared to be sure of step with a long staff held in his hands. The strangest thing they saw was that a huge Bald Eagle seemed to be guiding the way of this young man and his elderly follower. After the alarm was sounded and the Azteca soldiers ran towards the intruders, they suddenly stopped at the foot of the Great Temple. As they surrounded the two strangers and were about to strike them down, the eagle screamed and wildly flew back and forth over their heads as he spread his giant wings and displayed his huge, razor-sharp talons! They all looked on in horror and wondered if this was some sort of sign.

Just as the Aguila sentries had surrounded the two strangers, the elderly man held up his hands and waved them in circles in front of him as the huge bald eagle perched himself upon the elaborately engraved wooden staff. The young general looked on in wonderment and dismay. He thought to himself, "What manner of beings are they that there seems to be a protective aura about them?" Each time they approached, the Aguilas were somehow stopped and could go no further! They now just backed away. Not from fear but from what seemed to be a magical spell or something! Having positioned themselves to start striking at these strangers, the Aguilas were now told to "Stand Down" by the general.

"I beg you. Before you take any action, allow me to speak. We are here for a most special reason, and we have come in peace! My name is El Vision, and this is my son, Little Feather. He is here on a blessed mission that has been foretold for many, many moons, and I am sure that your emperor will welcome my son to meet with his!" The Azteca knights seemed to be transfixed upon the sight of these two strange people and the great eagle. To the Azteca, the eagle was a solar symbol that was very important to their religion. They felt the eagle was a warning or a spiritual omen, especially since their military order was symbolized by the eagle, a symbol of power, strength and greatness. This is when the Azteca general had left them and rushed up the stairs of the great temple to alert the emperor.

As the royal entourage proceeded and came closer to the strange visitors, Dificil and Little Feather were already communicating through their gift of mental telepathy. Now running and skipping down two stairs at a time, Dificil began to say, "I knew you were coming. I was anxious for your arrival. Do not fear, my dear brother, for I am here and no one will harm you!" "I am a little nervous, Dificil but not afraid. My father has raised me for this day, this prophesied time of our meeting and joining together! I have been anxiously waiting for us to meet and begin our new life together," exclaimed Little Feather.

At last, the grand meeting of prophesied lore! Now there was the presence of ancient spirits dancing in joy and celebration of this miraculous event, the friendship, the brotherhood of Dificil and his formidable protector, Little Feather!

As they all stood at the foot of the great pyramid, Dificil began to speak to his new friends, "Motlalia! Motlalia, (sit down), Little Feather and El Vision! Tlacuatia, atlia, auh atili atolli. (Give them something to eat, water and atole to drink." Atole (a drink made of rice). Dificil's guards and servants moved in a flash! Their eyes seemed to be ready to pop out of their heads! Who was this strange boy who had just arrived and yet was so familiar with Dificil? Why it seemed as if they were two lost brothers whom after years and years, were finally united! Dificil smiled and was overjoyed by the arrival of Little Feather and his father, El Vision!

"Tlahtli, nantli (Father, Mother), please meet my 'brother,' Little Feather!" Little Feather and El Vision dropped to their knees and bowed their heads at the feet of the "Tlahtoque" (nobles). Dificil's parents looked at each other in surprise and elation! They immediately felt a great sense of pride and wellbeing. Chichinotpotl, for some unknown reason, most strange to his psyche, knew that not only Dificil, but he, his wife, his whole kingdom, were suddenly safer and most definitely more secure. Now they were more stalwartly defended from not only enemies from the outside but also from inside dangers of treachery and deceit, due to the arrival of these two new friends who were now made members of the royal family.

Chichinotpotl told El Vision to rise and stand before them. As Dificil's father looked upon Little Feather's father, their thoughts coincided with each other, conveying the same sense of comfort and safety. Chichinotpotl placed his hand upon Little Feather's shoulder and bid him to rise also. As he did, the bodyguards moved towards him, but the great ruler raised his hand and exclaimed, "Let him be, he may look upon me. He and his Tahtli may face me and stand with me, the Empress Cuicani and Dificil. Henceforth, let it be known to all our people. Communicate this throughout the whole Kingdom, that I, the Great Chichinotpotl, have decreed, I have so ordered, that Little Feather and his Tahtli El Vision are now part of our family!"

Just as before when Dificil was atop the great pyramid, the earth was suddenly still. The sky was a beautiful violet blue, as was the color of his eyes, and there was complete silence all around. The birds did not chirp or sing, and not an animal stirred. The four winds were calm and silent, and all the people were subdued and found themselves filled with a profound feeling of happiness and glory! This was a historical bond!

Dificil smiled as he looked at Little Feather. He could see that he had twelve toes on his feet as well as twelve fingers on his hands, just like him! Little Feather gazed at the eyes of Dificil, all his eyes. This sight was just like his father said it would be. He felt numb with the realization that after such a long time, after so much training and preparedness, he was now finally at his place of destiny, alongside Dificil in the land of the gods! The home of Dificil, which was now his home, the capitol city of the Azteca, Tenochtitlan!

As the royal family looked out upon all their people, they heard the profound declaration from thousands of their loyal subjects, "Yectenehua! Yectenehua, Amehuantzitzin! Teotl! Teotl, Tecuhtzintli! Blessings upon you, Blessings upon you! Wonderful Lords!

Chapter Ten
"A Welcoming Home"

As they headed towards the royal palace, beautiful flowers were strewn before and after the royal entourage. When they passed in their brightly colored boats through the lovely waterways, all the Mexica (original name of Azteca), awed at the sight of this new, strange young boy and his father that sat alongside the great Chichinotpotl, the Empress Cuicani and the anointed one, Dificil! Along their path towards the palace, Little Feather gazed in wonderment at the greatest sight his eyes had ever seen! The most glorious vision of beauty, splendor, richness and grandeur! The great waterways of the magical city of Tenochtitlan! Why this was the city of gold that he had envisioned in his dreams. Cultured, colored, shaped, erected, molded and created explicitly as his father had told him. This passageway into Tenochtitlan was true testimony as to the advanced and miraculous engineering talents and techniques of the Aztecas. Little Feather was astonished by such majesty. He wondered if this place of such splendor was really Aztlan, (a magical, mythical place, et. el), "Heaven," and the origin of the Aztecas). All through the waterways, the shoreline brimmed with fruits, trees, plants and flowers. Every color imaginable was evident, and one could see such textured lines drawn in the dirt by the royal landscapers. Much of the plant life was visibly arranged in many different formations to illustrate and pay homage as sculptures and pictures to the many Azteca deities.

Gazing down into the clear blue water, Little Feather saw pools of thousands of multi-colored fish of many different sizes, some with tails, others with wings and still others with what looked like long snouts and horns. Huge tortoises mingled amongst the many huge pink birds, which were known as flamingos. As they fluttered their wings, they awoke the many brightly colored parrots that sat atop the huge trees along the causeway. Little Feather could not believe his ears when he heard them begin to speak not only in the Azteca Nahuatl language but in many other tongues as well. Dificil and Little Feather both roared with laughter when they saw how the skinny monkeys squealed playfully as they leapt from tree branch to tree branch and threw coconuts at each other that they had picked from the lovely palm trees. Little Feather thought to himself, so many creatures, so much life, this land was really blessed by the "Great Spirit."

He noticed that each water vessel was different in color. They were lavishly decorated and painted with drawings of animals, weapons and engraved writings. He was excited by the sight of such splendid culture and astounded by the realization that this was even more wonderful than what his father had described! On many occasions, while they sat by the campfire at night, El Vision told him of this unbelievable place! Now he was actually seeing it! Such greatness, such serenity, such splendor and grace! The land of the greatest warriors on earth! The land of the richest beings of the universe, whose scientific accomplishments and rich culture were already history and would be written about and spoken of for centuries to come! The empire of the gifted ruler of rulers!

The Nanas patiently awaited their great Dificil. It was time they knew for his daily wading and swimming in the royal pools, and then right after that, his warm bath and rest. Each NaNa was specifically chosen from a certain family who, from generation to generation, served as the personal caretakers, groomers and servants of the royal family. These NaNas were special in that they had the honor and privilege of personally attending to the Great Dificil! Thus, since birth, they were trained in the many methods and facets of performing such duties. Other than the two Supreme NaNas, each Nana was forbidden to marry and had to remain celibate all their lives. They could never be in the company of any male other than when performing their royal duties. Each NaNa was required to be perfectly groomed at all times with complete cleanliness. They all had to keep their hair length long, down to their knees. Flowers and decorative pins were allowed to be worn in their hair but no oils or other liquids could be used. Being of natural beauty, each NaNa kept her skin velvety soft and smooth, and unlike the maintenance of their long tresses, they were allowed to use sacred oils and scents created by the holy Teopixque upon their bodies. When a NaNa reached the time of her monthly menstruation, she could not appear in the presence of the royal family until her body function was complete and she was thoroughly clean. The two Supreme Nanas were the only ones who were allowed to marry, and their marriages were prearranged through the family "Capolli," lineage, so as to keep the same bloodline intact. If a woman chosen as a "Supreme NaNa failed in two childbirths to conceive another female, she and her husband were exiled from the kingdom, never to return again. Another NaNa from their lineage was picked as her replacement. Women chosen to be NaNas were kept isolated and lived together as a special group within the royal compound. They lived subservient lives but they were always protected by bodyguards and lived without want. Their own quarters were lavishly and richly adorned. They wore the finest of linen, silk and other refinements. They ate as the royal family ate, and they were allowed to be taught in the royal Calmecac schools just like the citizens and Aguilas of the upper echelon of society. Each NaNa's extended family was also well taken care of and received a generous monthly allowance and secured, comfortable living quarters.

Just before reaching the shore, after turning off the last inner waterway to the royal palace, Dificil was suddenly staring with a look of concern at Little Feather. As their minds met, he asked, "Little Feather, what's wrong, my dear brother? Your ears are folding first forward and then backwards, and the gills on each side of your face are appearing and then disappearing over and over! Is it that you feel the same as I do? Do you sense what I sense, danger?" Dificil thought to himself, "This is unbelievable. Little Feather only just arrived, and he already is feeling what I feel and sensing what I sense!"

Just then, another large water vessel painted in bright colors with drawings of deities pulled alongside the royal vessel. Both groups of passengers embarked from their vessels. The second boat carried the four noblemen of the supreme council. These high officials were the "Tlacochcalcatl", the "Tlaccatecatl, "The Etzhuanhuanco" and the "Tillancalqui." In the Aztec hierarchy, these men served as the Emperor's special council of advisors, and they were usually members of the same royal family. They were designated to be the next in line to succeed him if he was seriously injured in battle, or disabled through a sickness or disease or when he died.

As Dificil looked upon the Azteca nobleman, he felt a sense of misgiving, a strong force of evil. When Chichinotpotl stepped from his boat, Llore was already at his feet, growling at the Tlaccatecatl. Little Feather and Dificil suddenly jumped in front of the Tlaccatecatl and blocked his way as he was about to approach Chichinotpotl.

"Dificil, what game is this now? Why are you blocking the way of my great war chieftain?" asked his father. Both Little Feather and Dificil looked at each other as they reluctantly moved only slightly to the side. Dificil ordered Llore to sit still and let the Aguila commander approach Chichinotpotl.

The commander began to speak, "Greetings, my Lord, I would ask for an opportunity to sit and meet with you to discuss the finalization of our plans for our conquest in Guatemala." Chichinotpotl in turn, greeted the Tlaccatecatl and then said, "I appreciate your eagerness, my prized soldier, but at this time I must begin to make arrangements for a great celebration of the arrival of our most honored guest, members new, of our family!" "Whatever you wish, my Lord. I will await your summons so we can meet at a later date," he answered. The great commander bowed as the royal entourage entered through the huge golden doors of the palace before him. As they passed, he noticed the cold stares from both Little Feather and Dificil. He knew that this young boy and his new friend were not even remotely receptive to him. This being one of the few times that he had met the much-talked-of young son, he felt only coldness and a danger from Dificil. Llore was just watching him and looked like he was ready to attack him if he made too sudden a move! He thought to himself, "How could they know anything? Is it possible they anticipate my moves for the change of power and rule of our nation?

As they made their entrance Dificil and Little Feather stood close behind the great Chichinotpotl. After everyone passed through the huge doors, the commander and Dificil's elite Aguilas veered off to the other corridor towards the security holding area. El Vision was among the last to arrive and stepped from his boat. His eagle, "Itta," took off from the perch upon his staff and flew above the commander and his troops, following them every step of the way and watching closely!

After arriving in Dificil's private chambers, he and Little Feather talked about the feeling of danger they got from the presence of the Tlaccatecatl. They both agreed they did not trust him and that henceforth they would watch him and monitor all his activities very closely and when they spoke of him they would identify him as "El Raton," The Rat!

Chapter Eleven
"The Pools"

Step by step, inch by inch, slowly, Dificil crept towards the marble pool that was filled with volcanic water. Across the large room, all the way on Dificil's extreme right, Little Feather was smiling as he was doing the same. Their bodies shook with laughter as they continually teased each other. This new game was to see who would submerge himself into the pool first. Now they were both just standing in front of the glistening pools and ready to dive into the clear, hot water. It was so hot that steam could be seen rising from its surface! The NaNa's screamed as they watched both young boys dive into the water. They immediately followed the two boys into the pools, prepared to attend to them and apply the fragrant soaps to their young bodies. Dificil roared again with laughter as one of the older NaNa's fainted as she saw Little Feather's feet were now large fins, like those of the large tropical fish that swam around the royal palace. At each side of his head, suddenly long vertical openings appeared and seemed to cause bubbles to exit the side of his face! The NaNa's grew afraid and did not want to get close to him, and hurriedly exited the pool! Dificil called out to them and said, "Do not fear, what you see is only a natural transformation that takes place with my new brother when he enters the water. He is not only different, but special. Soon you will notice other "different" things about him and me, but you must not fear what you see nor should you reveal to anyone else outside of this palace what you will see. It is important that these things remain secret!"

Dificil smiled as he enjoyed watching Little Feather swim effortlessly beneath the clear blue water. He noticed how he would change speeds at various times and rotate his body. Dificil roared with laughter when the NaNa's screamed again as Little Feather came back up to the surface and water sprouted from both sides of his head! Dificil jumped from his pool into that of Little Feather's. They began to play with many different obsidian floating devices. Some of these just simply floated upon the water, while others strangely glided beneath the surface. The NaNa's patiently waited as the two boys continued to play and enjoy themselves. They admired the sleekness of their bodies and the awesome swimming ability each displayed. As Dificil lay back and floated upon the surface, resting himself, the senior NaNa exclaimed, "Your Highness, you must stop playing and allow us to wash you both. The time is close that your father will expect you and Little Feather to join them in the dining foyer. Please, Dificil, let us perform our duties and prepare you for "Mocochcayotia" (Nahuatl language meaning dinner). "Dificil, Dificil!" The senior NaNa grimaced as she watched him and Little Feather go underwater again because each time they did, they did not come back up to the surface for a long time! Finally, when she saw both their heads above the water, she was able to breathe, and her heart began beating again as her anxiousness and fear subsided. Trays of soft, fragrant soaps and oils were carried to the senior NaNa as she began to bathe Dificil. The other NaNas began to bathe Little Feather as well. Dificil playfully held out his arms as other NaNas softly scrubbed them with the soap-filled tropical sponges that were brought to the palace from the south. These sponges were orange in color, and their texture was as soft as silk. He lay back at the side of the pool and allowed them to attend to him. A rich aromatic shampoo was poured on his head as the NaNa's begged him to close "all his eyes." "We will most certainly suffer many lashings of the whip from your mother if your eyes should be hurt," they pleaded.

Dificil, always playing, finally closed his eyes and allowed the NaNa's to finish washing his pitch black, sleek hair. After washing his arms, back and chest, two of the NaNa's submerged themselves into the water and began to wash his lower extremities. Each of them softly washed his long legs in the front and back, on the sides and within his inner thighs. The senior NaNa closely watched them as they began to wash his thighs most enthusiastically, and while they began to cleanse his tepulli (penis). Water bubbles rose to the top from the gasps of air that exited the mouths of the NaNa's because they were shocked when they saw the length and girth of his most masculine tool! Suddenly, the senior NaNa slapped her hand down on both of the young NaNa's. "Enough, you have sufficiently cleansed Dificil down there! I fear you are spending too much attention and time upon his royal wealth," scolded the senior NaNa as she laughed too!

Flushed and embarrassed, both young NaNa's rose standing up in the water, requisite in the knowledge that their virginal lust was so evident!

All the while that Dificil and Little Feather were in the pools, Llore and Itta intently watched and listened, as their noses wiggled alerting their olfactory nerves to any faint or pervasive smells as El Vision opposite them at the front entrance of the parlor, was on guard armed with his keen sense of perception of any and all movement, and awesome hearing ability, abundant compensation for his lack of sight. Itta, the large bald eagle was at first perched atop the head of Llore and every once in a while moved his position for a better view and better listening. Llore was getting more and more agitated as the eagle kept moving and scratching his scull with its long, sharp talons.

"Why must you keep moving around over and over, as if you had fleas or lice or something?" Llore told Itta. "Why don't you stay still yourself, you breath so deeply that your whole body shakes, and you smell so bad as if you would rather remain here alone," Itta answered. Both Llore and Itta suddenly stopped bickering when they noticed the annoyed vibes they were receiving from El Vision. Through their telepathy, El Vision was communicating to them, "You must remain focused with your duties and concentrate on the great task at hand. We must be alert and ready, for danger as always is near!" The royal Aguilas that were also standing watch looked upon Llore and Itta, as they wondered at their steadfastness, their acute vigilance and their devotion to Dificil and Little Feather. They were told by Dificil's father, the great Chichinotpotl, that they should not interfere with the great white wolf and let him accompany Dificil anywhere he went. With the presence of Little Feather, the strange elderly El Vision and the great Bald Eagle, surely, no one would dare come close to the royal son or contemplate any strange or sudden move towards him!

The Aguilas, through their travels, had seen many different animals throughout the forests, the mountains and the wide plains, but never, not ever, had they seen a huge white wolf such as Llore. Why, when he stood up on his hind legs, he was at least two feet taller than they were. He was built with solid muscle and looked as if he weighed at least two hundred pounds with paws that were larger than their feet! Long razor-sharp claws stood out from those paws, and frightening, glistening, white fangs protruded from his powerful jaws. As soon as anyone came near Dificil or Little Feather, Llore would emit a loud, deep, hollow-sounding growl, which undeniably warned anyone of the sheer danger and their fatality if they came any closer. As he was summoned to do so by El Vision, Itta left his perch and began to slowly soar above the pool area, looking down on Dificil and Little Feather. El Vision wanted to make sure that they were totally safe. Both youngsters made him nervous as they continued to stay underwater so long. As the eagle would swoop down flying just above them, he could see Dificil and Little Feather beneath the surface, laughing and playing. He too observed how Little Feather's feet had changed to fins, and the "gills" on the sides of his head. He was pleased to see how easily and expertly they swam. The eagle listened to their conversations with them both, as did El Vision and Llore through their mental telepathy. They could tell how the two young boys were truly enjoying themselves.

It was apparent that they were indeed brothers, born to fulfill the Aztec prophecies and born to the earth to lead and save their people. Could it be that these two boys, with still so much to learn of life, could understand the ways of their kingdom, the importance of their heritage and the inherent dangers surrounding their task?

As they both exited the pools, they shook off the chill, causing Llore to instantly shake also. Seeing this, they both laughed and laughed as the Nanas quickly ran to dry them with soft towels and cover them with silk robes. As Dificil and Little Feather were dried and more soft fragrant oils were massaged into their young bodies, they spoke through their telepathic powers. They were already planning their midnight excursion outdoors into the wild, amongst their friends, the creatures of the night and free souls of the forest. They would be hiking through the valleys and mountainous pathways of nature, but for now, after a short rest, they must attend the ceremonious "Mocochayotia," (Dinner). The resonating sound of beating "huehuetls," (old traditional vertical drums) would soon be heard throughout the land as the many nobles, chieftains, and high-ranking warriors would dance a stately dance in their honor! The Nanas marveled at the apparent power, vigor and handsomeness of these two royal figures, and they beamed with pride of having the responsibility of caring for them! Dificil and Little Feather began to run as they raced each other in another contest. This one was to see who could reach Dificil's chambers first. As they finished their race with Dificil being the victor, they were laughing again. Out of breath, finally arriving to meet them there, the Senior Nana looked on in pleasure, to see her dear Dificil having so much fun and enjoying his new companion.

Dificil and Little Feather lay on their beds and were resting as the NaNas massaged them softly and hummed soothing songs to them. They both fell asleep for a while as the sun began to set, and a soft breeze swept upon them from an open window as they lay in a peaceful slumber. Itta sat perched just above them on a rafter as Llore lay at the foot of Dificil's bed.

The senior NaNa, after some time, walked back over to Dificil and rubbed his forehead softly and gently with so much love and whispered, "It is time to wake my dear prince. Dificil then slowly opened his eyes, all his eyes and smiled at his NaNa as she kissed him on his cheek. All the Nanas diligently began to prepare and dress them. They assisted them in donning their special attire for the dinner. Dificil and his father, being royalty, usually wore feathered suits. The Nanas laid out all his clothes for the evening, and among them his fantastic headdress. This was truly a work of art. Many painstaking hours had been put into the creation and assembly of this important piece for Dificil. The headpiece was composed of many eagle feathers sprouting up high. A gold band was at its base, which is how it was kept in place upon its bearer. His breastplate was made from buffalo skin, intertwined with specially picked reeds from the Chinampa fields and adorned with beautiful colors. The main color of Dificil's breast plate was green, for the picture of a green jaguar was placed at its center, the symbol of his royal lineage. His shield depicted a large bald eagle perched upon a snowcapped mountain as its beak gripped a large snake. His hair was partly braided and filled with bright yellow and green beads. He wore gold rings around his neck and wrist. His loincloth was of a tan color, which also had miniature pictures of jaguars painted on it.

His moccasins were sewn intricately with the threads of buffalo and lion hair, worn long from the point of his knees to the soles of his feet. Eagle talons embraced his upper arms. Even at this young age, it was amazing that such muscular definition was visible as seen from the bulge of his biceps, the thrust of his chest and the ripples of his abdomen. Little Feather too was elaborately adorned in a new jaguar uniform, silver in color, with attached red, white and green plumes sprouting from his military headpiece. He wore long deerskin moccasins upon his feet. His shield was also that of the jaguar warriors. He walked with a beautiful sword that was sheathed in a scabbard made of leather with studded pearls, rubies and obsidian.

"Te Tlacua, tlacualli nohuan"- (Come with me to eat), Dificil exclaimed excitedly to Little Feather. They both were now feeling very hungry and hurriedly walked out of their inner chambers and headed towards the corridor leading to the royal dining area, their bodyguards walking before and after them. Each soul that Dificil passed trembled, and they marveled at the sight of the young prince. "What matter of creation is this that upon entering the dining area, even the great Chichinotpotl stared in wonder at the majesty of his own, the Pilli, Dificil, the anointed Azteca!" Itta was well ahead, watching to prevent any sudden surprises, and Llore, as always, was at his side. El Vision, walking right behind them, felt the close bond that was already there between Dificil and his son. Together, they had embarked on a journey of untold wonders, their "ohtli" (way) was a path to dangerous and glorious adventures and a mission to avoid the foretold demise of the Azteca nation, the "Holocaust!"

Chapter Twelve
"Mocochcayotia"
The Dinner

When the royal family walked in, everyone had dropped to their knees with bowed heads. As Dificil and Little Feather entered the dining foyer following Chichinotpotl and the empress Cuicani, many of the people present noticed that they looked so much alike that they looked like twins!

Each guest stared in awe at Dificil's headdress, full of eagle feathers, flowing in the breeze from the huge fans that whirled above them atop the mosaic ceilings. Such an elaborately decorated reception area, it was filled with palm trees and a vast number of fragrant flowers lining the walls of the foyer. Flamboyant colors of the rainbow were reflected from the beautiful pools of water that ran adjacent to the huge dining tables.

As Dificil and Little Feather stopped at their designated place to sit, Dificil suddenly moved away, at the same time grabbing Little Feather's hand, urging him to follow. He went and stood next to his mother! He affectionately kissed her on her cheek and placed his hand on her forehead. The Empress Cuicani smiled, quite surprised, and at the same time, she sensed that this was some kind of blessing. This was another time when her son, though just a young boy, caused her to marvel at his unique spirit, his demonstration of love, and the fact that he was a special being. Dificil hugged her and said, "I love you, Mother. May the Great Spirit always protect you!"

After she and Chichinotpotl took their seats, everyone else was allowed to sit. As soon as Dificil and Little Feather sat down, they immediately began to play by kicking each other's feet beneath the table! While they played, Dificil recited something which seemed to be a song. "Little boys must laugh and play, little boys have much to say, their imaginations are so clear and abound, their insight is so gifted and profound and yes, they notice everything all around!"

Dificil observed the Tlaccatecatl ("El Raton"), seated a few seats to the left of him. Immersed in deep conversation with one of the young lady guests, El Raton didn't notice Dificil and Little Feather's watchful eyes upon him. He did not know that they were aware of the evilness in him. They already suspected him as an enemy with traitorous plans. Although the general did not see Itta perched on the rafter above him, he sensed something was dangerously close!

Llore sat adjacent to his feet beneath the table! As Dificil's mother watched her precious son play with his companion, she squeezed his hand and said, "My dearest son, there is a time to play and a time to eat. Please sit up and enjoy the feast that has been prepared for us." Dificil then accepted his plate from the senior Nana and began to feast on the delicious salad that had been first tasted for him by the head of his security team, a routine precaution to make sure that no one had poisoned his food.

As if on cue, Little Feather also began to eat his food and enjoyed the taste of such delicious greens and spices. They both laughed as they made crunching noises with their mouths while they ate. Dificil's mom just shook her head and smiled as her anointed son again continued to play. Little Feather's father, El Vision, was fully alert as he felt every movement of the Aguila General El Raton. The blind warrior remained stationed at the entrance door, just a few steps from the royal family, with the other members of the royal bodyguard.

Tray after tray of delicious food, fruit and other delicacies were presented to all as the gala dinner continued. After a while, the royal musicians entered the parlor, accompanied by exotic dancers, filling the palace with beautiful, glorious sounds and displaying expert, artful dances. Other performers conducted various feats of magic, tumbling, gymnastics and theatre. Such a grandiose spectacle, a wonderful occasion filled with laughter, happiness and contentment. Little did anyone know how close and how soon treachery and death were on the horizon!

CHAPTER THIRTEEN
"EVIDENT INTELLIGENCE, AND TIME TO LEARN"

As each day passed, the great Chichinotpotl watched his son in amazement. It was almost impossible for him to believe how quick he grew! Not only physically, but his mind, his advanced learning ability, his knowledge, his wit, his maturity! Chichinotpotl remembered the first day that he had taken his son to the holy temple. Just seven years old and yet he could exchange history, the past, the present and the future. Chichinotpotl recalled how all the Teopixque were seemingly mesmerized and hypnotized by his gifted son! How is it that his son knew so much about the earth, the sun, the moon, the four winds and the sky! How was it possible that this little boy could tell these holy men about their ancestors and their descendants to come? Dificil's Nanas also told the great ruler of the intelligence of his son. Bearing the responsibility to feed, bathe and generally care for him, day to day, the Nanas testified as to the uncanny ability of Dificil to memorize all his lessons so rapidly and easily. They told Chichinotpotl of his ease in learning other languages besides Nahuatl, his native tongue.

The Nanas also told him that somehow Dificil, Little Feather and El Vision seemed to communicate amongst themselves without speaking! All the younger Nanas didn't know that the Senior Nana also possessed the same gift, and all of this was already secretly known by Chichinotpotl and the Empress Cuicani.

After much contemplation and the strong urging of his wife and Dificil's Tlamatini, Chichinotpotl decreed that his son and his faithful companion Little Feather should immediately enter the "Calmecac" (The Aztec school of Nobility).

Chichinotpotl called his son before him and began telling him of his decision, "My dear son, everyone tells me of how smart you are and how quickly and easily you learn everything! Your mother and I are so proud of you, and I have directed your Tlamatini and other teopixque to prepare your studies in the Calmecac. You and Little Feather will begin your studies this week. Are you not happy with this new adventure?" With a broad smile and running up to his father, Dificil hugged him and said, "Oh, thank you, father! I have heard of the great lessons taught about science, mathematics, medicine, astronomy, and different languages, and so much more! Father, will I be taught also by those teopixque with the long hair?" "Yes, yes Dificil! Chichinotpotl laughed as he answered his son and thought to himself, he doesn't forget anything!"

He so ordered that the two should begin their studies of history and religion, the art of war and fighting techniques and the knowledge of different races and cultures of their land, all the people who were subservient to the Azteca. They would learn their different customs and tongues. They would learn of their strengths and weaknesses, their beliefs and habits. The two young boys would obtain firsthand knowledge as to other people's talents and expertise, their food, eating habits and their politics and forms of government.

Dificil was so happy and joyfully danced around the day that his father first told him that he and Little Feather would begin school. He earnestly prepared for the beginning of his studies. His beloved Tlamatini knew that he would not only be taught, but he would teach others.

Chapter Fourteen
"Preparation for School"

Chichinotpotl's decree was communicated throughout the land. His announcement was entered with great affair by the high priest in the Aztec annals, as it was such a great day that arrived in the history of the world! Dificil and Little Feather would begin their first day in the Calmeccac Academy! The proud mother and father of the gifted son had the servants prepare all that was needed for this occasion. The landscaping crews worked diligently throughout the night and placed all new, fresh floral arrangements along the path to the school, across the causeway, and upon the water vessels that would transport the great Dificil and his companion, Little Feather, to the Calmecac Academy.

Also, throughout the night, the Teopixque performed special holy services, praying before all the deities, for blessings to be afforded them both. Drums beat, chimes rang, and prayers were sung and hummed by the Teopixque within the holy order and all about the special temple, the Calmecac! Most intricate arrangements had been made by the royal Aguilas to ensure the anointed son, his father Chichinotpotl and his mother, the Empress "Cuicani" (the singer-name given the queen because with such a beautiful voice she always sang to the emperor and now Dificil), were totally protected and shielded from any unforeseen dangers.

The bright new day, the blessed academic beginning for Dificil, found the Nanas, busy laying out their soothing bath oils, aromatic fresh soaps and all the other fine toiletries they had for Dificil and Little Feather. As usual, while the Nanas patiently waited, they both splashed and played in the largest pool. Some of the Aguilas, who were also priests, grimaced every time the two boys climbed upon the holy sculptures. They would then dive into the clear water. Dificil and Little Feather laughed and laughed as they continued to play. Of course, nearby, Llore and the eagle Itta, as always, stood guard and watched them in bewilderment. How could they get so much enjoyment from just being in the water? Would not their skin wrinkle and lose color from being in there so long? As it was still early morn, the sun was just barely beginning to peak above the horizon.

The four favorite deities of Chichinotpotl, which were placed at each corner of the great pool, were still illuminated from within; these were the Tonatiuh, the (Sun God), Huitzilopochtli (God of War), Tezcatlipoca "Smoking Mirror," (Obsidian) and Quetzalcoatl, (feathered) Serpent Wind, symbol of Aztec Rulers. The Aztec engineers had carefully designed and built these figures utilizing their discovery of "Solar Energy." Each sculpture was made from a material that could absorb and store the heat and light from the sun. While Itta looked on, he could clearly see Dificil and Little Feather beneath the water, as the inner pool was also illuminated. Many bubbles were visible from the center of each pool. The centerpiece, which was placed at the bottom of each pool, was affixed within the pool walls through large holes on the side. This was part of the elaborate water cleansing filtration system built to ensure the prevention of bacteria and germs from forming in the water. The center pool had one hole in which fresh, cool water entered and still another in which old, warm water exited. Next to it was a smaller pool, which pulsed and its waves endlessly rotated in a circular current. This pool contained fresh, warm, volcanic water and was used to soothe and massage the body. The third and longest pool, specially built for Dificil's pleasure, contained a small waterfall at its mouth, dropping water down to a sunken array of small tunnels, hills and slopes in which a pair of beautiful, large dolphins swam. These were some of Dificil's favorite friends, with whom he and Little Feather loved to join in the water to swim and play.

Only El Vision, the senior Nana, Itta and Llore' through their telepathic powers, could hear as the two boys conversed with their seaward friends. Finally, Dificil and Little Feather got out of the third pool and reentered the center, smaller pool so the awaiting Nanas could bathe them. The younger Nanas could not help but laugh with glee as they watched Dificil swim underwater. Each one felt a stirring from their feminine loins as they watched Dificil's large tepulli trailing him as if it were a great, swollen snake! Each Nana with tender care washed and caressed Dificil's young, muscular body. Both boys aggravated the senior Nana because they wouldn't stop playing. The Nanas exercised so much effort to cleanse and prepare them for their first day of school. Each of their undergarments was laid out upon a gold-lined silk stool. Their outer garments and headdresses were held by Nanas waiting to finish dressing them. Each beautiful piece of clothing was brightly colored, mainly green, yellow and red. Gold wrist bands, finger rings of jade and head bands studded with rich rubies were given to Dificil and Little Feather by two other young NaNas.

For today, Dificil would wear his new long silk and leather moccasins. Tan in color with silver laces on the sides and bright gold lion hair adorning the upper portion. He wore his gold breastplate with the large green jaguar adorning the center. Dificil laughed so hard when he and Little Feather had finally exited the pool to get dressed. Just like every other time, the Nanas shrieked with fright as they witnessed how Little Feather's "fins" changed back to normal feet with his six toes, and the slits on the sides of his head disappeared as they dried him!

As he and Little Feather began to dress, they looked upon each other and began to plan their day. Through their mental telepathy, El Vision communicated to them that they would encounter numerous unusual events today at the school and that they may not have time to attend all their classes or meet all their teachers. The Teopixque had already prepared their curriculum and made sure every detail of their first day of school was in order. The Tlamatini planned all his duties with much apprehension and fear, for this was the first time that, when performing the holy rites, no human sacrifices had been offered to the deities! Chichinotpotl had followed through with the wishes of his son. He decreed that not one prisoner, not one human soul would be killed as a sacrifice to the Gods. The Teopixque feared the wrath of the Gods, but they feared Dificil even more!

CHAPTER FIFTEEN
"THE PROPHESIZED ARRIVAL OF THE AMAZON QUEEN"

As he and Little Feather walked with their escort to the school, he couldn't help but feel a reverberation, a sudden beckoning sound, some type of communication. As they drew closer to the temple, the sound increased in its intensity and clarity. Dificil realized that the sound that he was hearing was his name! Someone from within the temple was calling his name and crying out for help!

It was an urgent sound, a desperate call from a female seeking help not only for herself, but for her people and the chance of the survival of her kind!! Dificil realized that this was another telepathic connection. Who could be calling him through this means? Why he thought that Little Feather, El Vision, his senior Nana, and all the animals of the kingdom were the only ones that could communicate with him in this manner. As the Aguilas opened the huge, golden doors to the royal entranceway of the temple, Dificil saw on one side of the foyer a huge line of different tribes, "Calpolli" of Indians who had been taken prisoner. These poor souls had been captured in the latest conquest by the invincible Aztecs Warriors. Aligned by height with numbers emblazoned on their backs and chests, these prisoners stood naked but for just a thin loincloth wrapped between their legs, and most of the women stood with their breasts exposed to everyone's view. This seemed to be one of the last vile, shameful experiences thrust upon them at the hands of their conquerors.

Suddenly, all these prisoners began to pull on the chains that held their hands and feet. Even as they were whipped by the Azteca guards, they still all felt compelled to drop to their knees. All noise and movement ceased. Not a sound was heard as Dificil came up to the first prisoner in line. Dificil began to speak to this prisoner in a language foreign to all other Aztecas, the Mayan language "Quiche." This was the indigenous tongue of the Indians who knelt before him, who were captured during a battle in the southernmost region of South America. A place called Guatemala. No one knew that this prisoner would one day prove to be an important ally and a very valuable resource to help save their kingdom!

Taking his hand in his own, Dificil said, "Steady, I will not harm you. I am going to help you and see to your wounds." In shock, the Maya warrior raised his head and just nodded to Dificil.

Dificil could see scars across his chest and neck. He saw immediately that one of his hands was missing and that most of his hair had been burnt off. Dificil felt a pulling at his heart. He felt remorse and regret. He was filled with such a deep sympathy for this poor, defiled and injured creature before him. As everyone just looked on spellbound and afraid to move, Dificil placed his right hand on the man's head, and suddenly he had hair again and his burns disappeared! Everyone watching was in shock and could not believe their eyes. What did Dificil do? How did he heal that man? Dificil bid the prisoner to rise to his feet, and then he ordered the nearest guard to remove his chains. All this time, he still heard his name being called over and over again, and louder and louder!

Like everyone else present, Little Feather watched intently, astounded at Dificil's display of such tenderness, kindness and caring for another human being and his unbelievable ability to be able to heal wounds. He didn't understand why Dificil showed such generosity to just a stranger, a vanquished foe. Why should he care if this conquered Indio hurt or not? Oh yes, but maybe he did understand and realized again that this was the Great Dificil! The foretold ruler of the world who changed many normal, ritual procedures and military laws in the process of utilizing his own methods and ways of doing things!

Those close enough to hear, witnessed Dificil's ability to communicate with many of the calpolli in their own language! When he spoke, everyone was silent and just listened. When he suddenly moved, he would cause all others to stand still and pay attention! As Little Feather looked down the line of prisoners, he saw his father, El Vision, standing in the middle of this procession of strange souls. He too heard the sound, the reverberation, the voice! Following Dificil, he watched as the guards heeded his commands and released each prisoner from their heavy, spiked chains. Each one bore wounds and bruises all over their bodies. Some of their wounds were still open as droplets of blood spilled from their veins. Dificil continued to stop by each one and spoke with them trying to comfort them. Frightened, tired and confused, they now each held within them a ray of hope of survival! This young prince before them, unlike any other foe they had ever encountered, showed them mercy and, yet at the same time, displayed great strength and commanding respect just by his presence.

Suddenly, Dificil stopped in his tracks! He stood still and stared at the most beautiful creature he had ever seen in his young life. It was the source of the sound of the reverberation! This is where the voice came from! Alas, it was you, "I could speak to you without opening my mouth, and hear your response without using my ears."

This young woman was dressed only in a torn uniform of some sort. She had long, brown, shiny hair with blond streaks at the inner sides. He was stunned by the sight of her large, ruby red lips. They seemed to be so moist and succulent! Aye, but those fiery, bewitching eyes! They appeared to be as green as the vast grasslands that surrounded his kingdom, yet red as hot molten fire when she dared to look at him! Her skin was olive in color but with a darker hue. So soft, as silk, and so tender as that of a newborn baby! Dificil could not help but notice the lovely shape of her breast that looked to be about to bust free from her torn dress. They appeared to be so perfectly shaped, round though somewhat oval, with almost all their abundance in full view. The top portion of her dress barely covered any part of them. So young and yet totally inexperienced as a man, Dificil felt the urgent, immediate need to be near her! He felt a tremulous stir in his loins as he began to sweat profusely because a sudden fever seemed to overtake him! Her long legs were beguiling and tempting even as they were scratched and bruised. Her feet were small, and her toes were curled as those of a koala bear that Dificil had seen drawn in the historic annals by the nomadic Teopixque. As he looked into her eyes, he saw anger and defiance, but they also reflected a deep softness and tenderness that he felt emanated from her very soul! Somehow, he had the feeling that he already knew this Amazon warrior. As she stood amongst the other group of strange women, Dificil was told by one of the Aguila generals that she was the leader of this group of warriors who had been captured in the Azteca's southern conquest. She was an Amazon Queen. "And what would your name be," Dificil asked of the lovely, wild warrior.

Patiently waiting for a response, she finally answered Dificil in a beguiling voice that sounded like it was coming from clouds, "Consuelo" she answered. It was a name meaning comfort. He felt that meeting her indeed brought him great comfort! As the chains were removed from the other Amazons, Consuelo looked at her warriors; she and they all suddenly fell to the floor, flat on their faces. This was their display of complete reverence and homage to this Aztec prince. She looked up again at him. By the Gods! His eyes! Those eyes! Consuelo's mind, her soul exclaimed! She realized immediately that Dificil was "The Chosen One," she had been told about. The only being in her whole life that she felt she could ever feel subservient to. Being a little older than Dificil, she had already experienced battle and fought many foes. Never before did she feel she should or could put her anger, her fierce aggression, in check, but now her natural instinct to rebel and attack was involuntarily put to a stop!

As the Amazon queen and Dificil continued to stare at each other (she not knowing the edict that no one could look at Dificil directly), El Vision quietly and softly approached Dificil and knelt before him, requesting permission to speak. Dificil, with a strange, benevolent look upon his face, turned towards El Vision and told him to rise to his feet. Smiling, he grabbed El Vision's arm and said, "You and Little Feather are family now, and we are as one. You must not hesitate to approach me. Please speak and tell me what I want to hear!" Slowly, he began to speak and asked, "Shall I have the Aguilas escort the Amazon Queen and her bodyguards to your palace so they could have their wounds attended to and then have the opportunity to cleanse themselves in the palace pools? I could then see that they are properly fed and allowed to rest."

"I thank you for your most kind attentiveness. You apparently have been reading my mind! I believe you already know that this Amazon is not just another stranger to our kingdom, nor will she ever be. You will have my Nanas attend to her personally," commanded Dificil. El Vision motioned to Consuelo to follow him. She and her entourage bowed again before Dificil and then proceeded to follow El Vision's lead, exiting the Calmecac temple.

Shaking his head in disbelief and horror, an Aguila general who was secretly watching Dificil's every move, turned and left the temple too. He was shocked by such a demonstration of kindness by Dificil to the enemy warriors. He hurried to tell the chieftain, El Raton of Dificil's latest exploit! Unbeknownst to him, overhead following closely was the great eagle Itta as Llore, Dificil's wolf, stood back and patiently waited at his master's side. Tonight, Dificil, El Vision and Little Feather would receive another report of the evil, treasonous plans being made against him, his father and their kingdom from their invisible spy, the great eagle Itta. Dificil felt sadness with the realization that there were traitorous Azteca like El Raton, and that not all his people loved him and wished him well! He was saddened also because he knew he would personally have to raise his hand, utilize all his strength and power soon, to eliminate his enemies. His heart felt kindness, but his alert mind and defensive instincts warned him that in the immediate future, he would have to act with cunning and deadly, swift action against all those who dared to threaten him, his people and his kingdom!

CHAPTER SIXTEEN
"LESSONS TAUGHT, LESSONS LEARNED"

Dificil continued to watch the Amazon as she and her entourage followed El Vision out of the Calmecac temple. Slowly, the fever that he felt when she was beside him subsided, and he again began to focus on his task at hand. He began to look upon the different calpolli of captured warriors and their poor physical condition. These people were brought to Tenochtitlan from the farthest southern regions of Mexico. They all spoke in different tongues, and yet he was still able to communicate with them! Amazing! Here before him were chiefs, warriors and priests of calpolli such as Chalcas, Tlaxcalans, Huexotzingans and the Mayas.

All this time, Chichinotpotl was just standing by as he observed everything that took place. He saw the look in Dificil's eyes, the sudden change in his demeanor and the apparent bewitching spell that came over his son when he met the Amazon Queen. He knew his son's heart had just been stolen by such a beautiful, female warrior queen. After the Amazon left, Chichinotpotl went up to his son and placed his hand upon his shoulder, trying to calm him down. He could feel violent tremors going through his body and, with a knowing smile, understood Dificil's amorous reaction upon meeting the Amazon Queen. He then said, "My precious son, I know and could tell what you feel. Please return to the rest of the world that surrounds you! I myself experienced the very same soul-searching transformation that took over my very being when I first met your mother. You must now try to relax, calm yourself and breathe deep! Hearing the words of the Emperor, El Vision himself could not help but smile too, for it was quite evident to him that such an amorous reaction from the Pilli had taken place."

You must complete the task at hand, for it is time that you begin your classes as your teachers await your attendance. Please do not be too troubled about these prisoners either, for they are merely suffering the consequences of what happens to those who oppose our people. These captives are warriors who tried their best to defeat us and end our way of living, our ability to grow, prosper and gain more territory. We will always need to expand to new regions to allow for the continuous growth of our nation. We must maintain our strength and fight to survive. Pilli, I see the sad look upon your face and know that it is because your inner spirit is filled mostly with peace, love, and serenity. Those are true qualities that you were born with, and that is good, but you must also accept and learn to live with the "dark side" of reality. "You are the anointed son, the future ruler of the Azteca. You will soon learn more about the necessity of war, the right of conquest and our destiny to rule the world," declared the emperor.

"This is why I have decided that at such an early age, you begin your studies, research and physical training. I too, studied at a very early age through the Calmecac. It was my father, your grandfather, who saw the need for me to learn the many tongues of the many different people of our land. He made sure that I understood the studies of math, science, astronomy, geography and medicine. He personally trained me as I will you, in the many martial defenses, the use of weapons, navigation and battlefield strategies. You must be patient, receptive and attentive, for you have much to learn and little time, I fear, to prepare for what seems to be a most uncertain future. I am confident that you will be ready, for as you have already communicated to me through your visions and dreams, perilous days and much danger are on the way! Dificil understood the reality of all that his father had said! He realized that most of his childhood thoughts and innocence were at an end. He understood that yes, there would be death in the future! There would be killing, dying, and war, and he would be directly involved and would have to not only order such death but personally raise his hand and kill other humans himself! This he would have to do to protect his family, his friends, the Azteca and the future of their world!

As he and Little Feather stepped through another huge door into a large classroom, their bodyguards moved away from them and stood alongside an adjacent wall. Both the young boys stared in awe at the huge colored solar lamps that were hung on the walls. Many scrolls were piled on large shelves as the nervous, learned teachers with heads bowed, awaited a signal to begin explaining and describing these "Geographic" teachings to the two young boys. Dificil noticed the pointed wooden sticks that a few of the Teopixque held in their hands, down at their sides. Dificil figured that these sticks were used by them to point to certain configurations on the maps. The Teopixque didn't move their hands, which held the "pointers," until given permission from the head priest to begin. This was necessary because they knew that with the presence of Dificil or anyone from the royal family, any sudden movement, especially in the direction of him, could be deemed as a threat and the Teopixque would be killed instantly.

Upon receiving the signal, the Tlamatini started describing the land to Dificil and Little Feather, pointing out their present location at the Calmecac, set in Tenochtitlan, their homeland, their kingdom. As the priest continued on with his lesson, he described the mountainous regions, the lakes, waterways and swamplands to the east. He explained how travel was conducted through the many causeways, forests, and mountain paths to their great city of Tenochtitlan. The priest pointed out the different locations of where certain wild animals and livestock lived and bred, and where different vital materials, precious stones and herbs and spices came from.

The Tlamatini described the "Chinampa District" that was located around the southern lakes. Artificial islands were made by filling the lake with soil by many farmers who worked and cultivated this area as resident tenants and laborers. This process is how much of Tenochtitlan was created and developed, and this is how much of the food was supplied to Tenochtitlan. The priest went on to tell how a sophisticated drainage system was installed, including dams, sluice gates, and canals and thus throughout the Chinampa zone, was how this water-controlled system was interconnected.

"My father told me of the construction of a big system of aqueducts to bring water from the mountain springs to our towns, but I must say I still do not understand some things about the water systems. What amazes me is how they could get water to travel up and down in the palaces as high as two and three levels," exclaimed Dificil. As he said this, he couldn't help but smile when he looked at Little Feather, remembering how they both enjoyed so much fun the day before when they were draining all the toilets in the palace over and over again. The empress Cuicani was so aggravated because when she made them stop doing this on one level, they just ran up to another level and started all over again! Waiting patiently again for their attention, the Tlamatini continued by saying how all the Azteca were proud of their engineers who had developed all this land and had accomplished such intricate and complicated architecture and engineering.

Concentrating on what he was hearing as he was looking upon the various displays and sculptures of "Tlaloc, the God of all water, from all sources," Dificil suddenly spoke, "My dear priest, you have told us of the genius of our engineers. I too am awed at such accomplishments, yet at the same time, you have described the many climatic, deadly floods that have taken place throughout the years. There has been much destruction and loss of life due to our inability to prevent such flooding. Why haven't our engineers built other dams and additional support systems to prevent such devastation? Could the engineers not have developed a means of flood prevention and, at the same time, created ways to harness the awesome power of these waters to better serve us? These waters could be used more efficiently as sources of additional power and energy." The old Tlamatini marvelled at the intelligence and gifted observations of Dificil! Bowing again before Dificil and Little Feather, the priest exclaimed, "My dear anointed one, your observations and creative ideas are profound and ingenious. With your permission and that of our ruler, Chichinotpotl, plans will be made to begin the creation of such important changes to our water systems. Dificil smiled at Little Feather as he conveyed to him through their mental telepathy that they also could have more waterfalls and pools built for their play and enjoyment!"

As the priest continued with his lesson of geography, Little Feather noticed numerous errors in the markings and names of pueblos, forests, and mountain ranges on the colorful maps. He respectfully informed the elder priest of the correct markings and other descriptive names.

Dificil again began to address the Tlamatini, "Please forgive the interruption, but I would like to respectfully point out some of the errors in the information you have given us thus far."

"Upon listening to your description of the mountains in the region of Monterrey, I must inform you that the mountain ridge you named 'Sombra'(the shadow) is named as it is shaped, 'La Silla' (the Saddle). Not all of the crops that are planted and harvested in the valley are cotton; apparently, you forgot to mention that we also have an abundance of wheat and maíz (corn). The region that you have displayed as being just north of Vera Cruz is inhabited by Mayas, not Psuite, and the language spoken is Quiche. I also see on the maps displayed that you have a lot of figures depicting many lions in the forest to the east of

Tenochtitlan. Actually, there are twice that amount within the forests to the west," exclaimed Dificil. He didn't mention that he learned of this during the first few nights he began to sneak out and visit with all his animal friends of the forests.

Little Feather added, "The water currents from the river that run through the east forest flow towards Tenochtitlan, not away from it, as it is just the opposite of the water flow of the forest to the west."

As he continued listening to the teachings of all the Teopixque Dificil observed closely all the facial and body characteristics of each one. Like the Teopixque he met in the Holy Temple, they all wore their hair very long, which is why some of them had their hair down to their knees! They were very thin but muscular, and their facial expressions always seemed to be so serious. Through their mental telepathy, both Dificil and Little Feather agreed with their observations. "Would you like your hair to be that long someday? If your hair was that long, you would look like a huge oak tree with all its many leaves," laughed Dificil. "All of them are so skinny, and I wonder if they ever eat," added Little Feather, as they both laughed aloud.

"Tonight, we will venture into the forests and enjoy the clean, fresh air and the company of all our many animal friends, but now that my father knows of my 'nightly excursions,' we must also have the company of our Aguila bodyguards," Dificil told Little Feather. "El Vision, I would like you to join us so I could show you many of our wonderful friends that no one else knows about who live in the forests. Though your eyes may not see, I'm sure you will be able to smell and feel many of these beautiful and exciting creatures. You can also touch the different growths and textures from the huge assortment of plants and trees," Dificil concluded.

As he stood nearby, the Aguila general who gave daily reports about Dificil and his doings to El Raton looked on, confused. He listened to the critique of both Little Feather and Dificil and thought to himself that it was blasphemy on their part to correct one of the highest priests. At the same time, he was confused because for one instant the two young boys conversed with the Teopixque, then they suddenly stopped and were smiling at each other. They continuously nodded their heads and seemed to be talking to each other, even though no words were spoken. How could that be? What kind of human beings were these two boys, anyway? Surely El Raton will want to hear of this, the Águila thought to himself.

Dificil grew tired and felt he needed to step away for a while to relax. Along with Little Feather, he walked out into the hallway. Just then, a very young girl passed by them. As she passed by, accompanied by her mother, she looked upon Dificil and her eyes widened to fullness and sparkled. She looked into the eyes of Dificil, all his eyes. A soft smile appeared on her face and as Dificil gently touched her hand and said, "I know, little flower, you recognized me right away! I am Dificil, and you are a beautiful angel filled with more of the Azteca spirit than anyone will ever know! Your future is meant to be part of mine, for you will save us all from one of the worst traitors there could be, one of our own military leaders! Your talent will be that of having the ability to speak in different tongues. Your power will come from patience and listening. Your destiny will be to warn us of danger and treachery." This was the communication instantly exchanged between Dificil and the young female Azteca named "La Salvadera." Actually, this young girl was the daughter of an Azteca merchant family known as "Pochteca" (long-distance merchants). The position of Pochteca was an occupation that could only be inherited, and she was also already being trained to serve at the same time as a "Naualoztomeca" (a disguised merchant), who served as a trader-spy. These people infiltrated other lands and transformed themselves completely by imitating the indigenous peoples. They wore their hair the same way, they dressed in the same clothes, and they spoke in the same language to blend in as natives of that country. The Pochteca were so important that they were, at times, publicly acclaimed by the ruler in Tenochtitlan. La Salvadera was one who would become especially close to Dificil and the royal family. At a very young age, through her family, she had been personally appointed by Chichinotpotl himself to begin her training as Dificil's future Pochteca.

He foresaw her gifts of intelligence, cunning and dedication and decided that she would indeed serve him, Dificil and their kingdom as a most valuable asset!

Chapter Seventeen
"Consuelo, A Special Being"

As he slowly walked away from the pool area and proceeded through the royal lodging chamber, El Vision still could feel her presence; he could smell her feminine fragrance, and her essence filled the air. Even though she was dressed raggedly from her previous fighting and long journey, and even though she was bruised, sore and somewhat dirty, there was still a freshness that emanated from her body. El Vision exclaimed to himself, "I can't blame Dificil for being so profoundly moved by this Amazon queen! She exudes sensuality, and there is warmth and an aura of magnetism about her. Such a beguiling creature, she surely is someone special. She indeed fits the description of Dificil's foretold special companion, the future Empress of Tenochtitlan! Why her way, her intense character, her majestic being dare I say, seems as if she is 'Chalchiuhtlicue,' ('She of the Jade Skirt'), the deity connected with the worship of groundwater)."

As she removed her scant clothing, the other Amazons stepped back and permitted the Azteca female to continue to attend to their queen. Consuelo followed the senior Nana through the narrow corridor and suddenly felt refreshing cool water falling upon her from the ceiling. These showers of water that pulsed and penetrated her soft skin began to soothe her and make her once again feel fresh and clean. As they continued to walk through the cavernous walkway, additional jets of water began to spray upon her from the sides of the walls. She suddenly noticed strange serene-sounding music all around her. She heard the beat of soft drums, the chimes of distant bells and the silk resonance of harps and other string instruments! As her entourage was allowed to follow and enjoy the same revitalizing ministrations, they wondered at such sublime, advanced and exquisite creations of the Azteca! Upon reaching the end of the corridor, Consuelo and her ladies were led to the largest pool. Their bodies shuddered as they began to feel the wonderful warmth of the volcanic water, the "Temazcalli" (steam bath).

Consuelo, with a soft, relaxed voice, declared to the other Amazons, "This is within the realm of greatness, splendor, and magic that we were told about. There could not be any other wonderful state of being or other world created by the gods!"

When they entered the pool, they noticed the presence of the other Nanas and her entourage suddenly surrounded their queen, but then they somehow immediately knew there was no threat of danger as Consuelo raised her hand and commanded her warriors to stand back and relax. She told them that there was no need of a defense when one was surrounded by such beauty, such serenity and such kind catering from Dificil's own learned and gifted female comforters. As she completely relaxed for the first time in "many moons," Consuelo enjoyed the wonderful fragrance of the soft shampoo that the senior Nana rubbed in her long hair and enjoyed the exotic scents of the multi-colored soaps the other young Nanas offered her. She asked the senior Nana, "Is this the Aztlan that we have been told about? I feel as if I am in a paradise, created just for me!" She slowly washed her face, then the other Nanas softly scrubbed her arms and her sore elbows with fluffy sponges. It had been so long since she felt so special and so cared for. She laid back and allowed the young Nanas to continue to wash and soothe her aching body.

As a leafy floatation device was placed beneath her, she relaxed even more than she thought she should, but then she knew she was now in Dificil's world. She was now welcomed in his domain and protected. As she started to doze off into a restful sleep, she suddenly sensed something, someone, why it was Dificil! He was calling her through their mental telepathy and told her all was well, all was well! "Don't fear, my dear friend, just rest and relax. Tomorrow will bring us not only a new day, but an opportunity to learn more of each other, and I feel a great new adventure." Dificil declared.

As Consuelo peacefully slept, she began to dream strange dreams, yet dreams that she seemed to recognize as sights and sounds from the past, or were they visions of the future? She saw herself with Dificil and Little Feather, accompanied by Llore and Itta. She saw them as one, together, united and powerful. As her body floated upon the water, she felt as if she was amongst the clouds, within the heavens and with the gods. She saw Dificil and Little Feather as "Coatl," (Aztec meaning serpent or twin).

Ah, but those eyes! all his eyes surely set him apart from any other man or creature here on this earth. What caused her feelings to abound with such great passion all of a sudden as he came near? Why did she begin to perspire and tremble? Why did her legs seem to fail her and cause her to feel like she would fall?

Was it fear? No! She feared nothing or no one! Was it dread? No, she immediately sensed a feeling of relief and redemption as Dificil had placed his hand upon her shoulder. Then what was this profound, strange and wonderful feeling that she felt at the presence and touch of him? She knew not the answer, only that she was hypnotized and entranced by his presence! This strange feeling seemed to come from her very soul, and somehow she knew that henceforth her life, her whole world would evolve around him! As her bodyguards looked upon their great queen, they too relaxed and relished the warm water, the soft soaps and oils and the great attention placed upon them by Dificil's young Nanas. Never had they experienced or enjoyed such lavish luxury and pleasure.

The same thing was on their minds at the same time! "This must truly be the land of the gods, the land that their queen had told them about many times before. Yes, indeed, this must be the place the Aztecs called 'Aztlan?' They didn't know for sure, but it was beautiful! It was magical! This was the world of Dificil!"

CHAPTER EIGHTEEN
"WOMEN TO WOMEN"

She suddenly awoke as she felt the soft touch of the senior Nana's hand upon her forehead and heard her soothing voice, "Awake, dear queen, we should move from here now, so that you could retire to the bed chambers and rest. You must prepare yourself for tomorrow's banquet. I myself have picked out an array of different types of clothing that you may choose from. The clothing comes in many different colors. The material comes from different parts of the world, woven into luxurious, exotic apparel." Upon entering the private bed chambers, Consuelo could see that the NaNa had also laid out variations of jewelry that she could wear.

Consuelo was awed at such luxury, such beauty and such craftsmanship of the seamstresses who had made these clothes. She gently touched each fabric. She felt each piece of clothing and pressed a silk gown to her skin. It felt so soft and elegant!

"Consuelo, I want you to look at these clothes and decide on what you would like to wear. These garments are unique and very special, and it's evident that they were meant for you! I have heard the talk of the Teopixque who have seen you. Dificil's Tlamatini told me that you are the woman who was written about, and your arrival was foretold many years ago. The holy teopixque say that you must be the goddess of fresh water,

"Chalchiuhtlicue." That is why if you look closely, each garment bears an insignia, a picture or engraving of objects typifying rivers, lakes, streams, and all other forms of fresh water. When you are seen tomorrow with Dificil and the royal family, everyone will know instantly that you are special," added the NaNa. "But my kind lady, I don't feel worthy of wearing any of these fine clothes, they seem to be apparel and adornments of the Gods!" Consuelo declared.

To don this special apparel is not only my request, but it's an order handed down to me from the great Chichinotpotl and thus, I beg you to please comply. It would not be good to disappoint the emperor," exclaimed the Senior NaNa. Consuelo nodded her head, consenting to this request from the kind lady and moved toward the bed so the young NaNas could begin to put the beautiful evening wear on her and prepare her for a quiet night of rest. As the young women attended to the Amazon queen, the senior Nana noticed the far off look in her eyes. The NaNa could see that Consuelo was in deep concentration. Encouraging the Amazon to speak openly, she said, "Please just ask the questions that are on your mind."

Consuelo began by saying, "I confess much nervousness and apprehension in meeting the royal family. I have only just recently arrived here in Tenochtitlan and as a former adversary, it is amazing to me that I would be allowed to be in the same room with them, much less accompany them to the royal dinner!"

"Young lady, you have met Dificil. He demonstrated his wish for you to be with him and his family. I don't think anyone could deny the instant amorous connection you two have made, especially the Emperor and Empress. Your uniting is prophecy and a blessing to all of us! Please do not be afraid and do not hesitate to accept the welcome you have received. I am sure you have many questions about the royal family and particularly Dificil," concluded the NaNa.

"Oh my gracious friend, your perception of my thoughts and feelings are true! May I say that never before have I been so profoundly affected by the presence of a boy, a man, a male human being! You must know in our culture males are mere subjects we use as slaves and for breeding. Truly, this person is so very special and blessed. His strength, his vigor, his intelligence, is so evident! I believe anyone would be apprehensive in his presence. He radiates an aura of power and majesty and at the same time you could feel the warmth and kindness of his very soul, could it be that I was having such a terrible nightmare and it suddenly turned into such a splendid dream? I must confess that the instant Dificil was next to me all manner of hate, anger, and retaliation left me. No longer did I feel I had to be on guard and alert, expecting danger. I felt a sudden comfort, relaxation, and safety in his presence! Oh, dear NaNa I must also reveal to you that I felt such a strong attraction, an acute need to be near him. To look into his eyes, all his eyes and be able to communicate with him and hear anything he wanted to say. To answer any inquiry or request that he might make and to just simply say, YES! My heart pounded mercilessly in my chest when he placed his hand upon my shoulder! I felt a sudden, strong urge to take hold of him and cling to him! NaNa, please tell me that what I am feeling is not just a fantasy, not just a wonderful dream. With his touch, my whole body was filled with a burning fire! My very nerves rattled at such a rampant beat, as if there were a thousand war drums pulsing in my body! I couldn't help but feel such steaming warmth upon my thighs that my legs felt as if they would melt and crumble. I felt a sudden urgency within my very core, and all the time I knew that henceforth, I would be totally consumed by him and be as a soft flower petal within his strong hands," exclaimed Consuelo.

"My dear young queen, may I first say that there is nothing wrong with the feelings you have just described to me, nor am I surprised at this happening. Many moons have gone by since scribes, scholars, and Teopixque began foretelling of this coming to pass. Dear child, what you are experiencing is just the beginning of a long journey into the world of Dificil! Your meeting is not mere chance, but a prophecy! You were blessed in that your star in the sky directly aligned with his. Your whole world from now on will be centered on the life of Dificil! Take heed to the lessons that will come from him. For he is the anointed one and you must love, protect and care for him always, even at the cost of your own life, if necessary," concluded the senior NaNa.

It was quite apparent to Consuelo that this was one of many times she would meet with the Senior NaNa. She experienced a complete transformation, seemingly to her very soul, and her life now belonged to Dificil, and she was now part of his world!

Tomorrow she would enter into the grand dinner with the royal family, with Dificil! For now, she felt that she should rest if she could, but could she? So much excitement! So much wonder! Consuelo realized that she was brought from the throes of death, defeat and despair, only to suddenly be saved, at peace and gloriously happy to be with Dificil!

CHAPTER NINETEEN
"NIGHT AIR"

The night was so clear, the air so pure, and a faint scent of rain was upon the land. The forest was so dark and only now, so quiet! Dificil, Little Feather, El Vision, Llore and the Itta all stopped and looked upon the wonderful night sky. It was such an amazing sight, so many bright stars. As they continued to lead, flanked and followed by the Aguila bodyguards, Dificil and Little Feather continued to count the stars and skip and hop and jump along on their merry way.

"Do you think if we really ran at full speed that the Aguilas could keep up with us?" asked Little Feather. "Why, you're the one who has feet that turn into hooves, and you're asking me," exclaimed Dificil. This may be true Dificil, but your feet seem to never touch the ground when you're running! Well then, shall we race towards the clearing ahead and see who gets there first? All the animals followed and basked in the glory of enjoying the company of the great Dificil and his friend! Dificil laughed aloud because just as he had said, he watched Little Feather's feet turn into hooves! He himself moved so gracefully and silently. It was true, El Vision noticed he didn't hear the sound of Dificil's feet touching the ground!

As El Vision followed both boys as closely as possible, he could tell that Dificil's body moved with the sleekness of a gazelle, his strides were as strong as those of a jaguar and as silent as the movements of a viper!

The Aguilas grimaced in pain as they struggled to keep up with the young boys! Their freshly lit torches didn't help them navigate very well through the brush and all the trees. Sometimes they stumbled and fell after running into a tree. Every time that this happened, Dificil and Little Feather yelled out to the Aguilas to remind them teasingly, "Ando Ciego!" "Ando Ciego!" and just as quickly, the bodyguards transformed their concentration and movements with "Ando Ciego." As they continued on with such an arduous task, they were stunned by the speed and the agility of both Dificil and Little Feather. Dutifully, the Aguilas struggled to keep up, for it was their mission to make sure that there were no dangerous surprises as they protected the most prized being of the Universe!

All of a sudden, there was a clearing and a bright light. Why, it was a bright star which seemed to be directed upon a lurking creature in the bush! What was that! It looked like something huge and black. At first, all they could see was two bright, shiny, eyes. It was a jaguar! The jaguar moved with such speed, taking huge leaps and bounds and powerful, long strides in their direction! The Aguilas struggled to catch up to Dificil and protect him! Llore was already in front of Dificil, rushing towards the attacking jaguar, as Itta began to speed down upon the jaguar with his sharp talons poised to tear at the huge animal! Little Feather threw himself in front of Dificil to shield him! Dificil yelled out for Llore to stop and for the eagle to cease its descent upon the black cat! He pulled Little Feather aside and stood before the huge jaguar alone! The jaguar stopped in his tracks, landing on all fours and then lowered his head. The fierce animal grunted and seemed to gasp for air. Everyone else stopped too! No one moved and all stood still, mesmerized by the miraculous power Dificil demonstrated over this animal. One of the most powerful and feared creatures known to man! The blazing eyes of the jaguar then looked upon Dificil. Not with the devilish, evil, mean look it had at first, but now with a look of submission and fear! Dificil began to pet this scary animal as the jaguar now seemed relaxed, contented and at peace. Everyone could hear a sound coming from the jaguar; he was cooing and purring! How could this be? How could this happen? This animal was the most feared of all the animals on Earth! This huge" Mizton" (Nahatl language meaning cat) usually hunted man himself at his leisure, and now here he was, the same creature lying down, totally submissive at the feet of Dificil! Dificil began to speak to the "Mizton", "No imacai, No imacai, (don't be afraid). "Axitia, Axitia, Axitia, icniuhtli! (Come closer and accompany me this night, my dear friend!"

All those around Dificil bowed before him and praised his name! Again, another situation presented itself as proof he was a most unique and godlike being! Dificil smiled and petted the jaguar again as he marveled at the sight of the powerful-looking creature. Dificil put his own hands on top of the jaguar's paws. "Look, Little Feather. His paws are about three times the size of one of my hands! The burly animal continued to softly purr as Dificil applied "Sanas" (rubbing and soothing) to his large head and powerful back. "Go on, my dear friend! We will leave you at peace now to continue your reign over the jungle and the forest. May the Great Spirit be with you and keep you safe!" Slowly, the fierce cat rose and walked away backwards, not turning his back to Dificil, and then he disappeared into the bush.

The young leader of the Aguila bodyguards approached him, bowing on his knees. "My dear lord, it has been a long time since we began this outing. Would it not be advisable for us to return to the palace?" Dificil was a little tired from all the excitement and realized that he and Little Feather had really put the Aguilas through a lot, and they were probably exhausted. He said, "I believe you are correct, my general. I do feel we should rest awhile. But we shall make camp here, for I'm not ready to return to the palace just yet. There is another place I want to visit." "Whatever you wish, my lord," answered the young general. Immediately, some of the Aguilas began gathering kindling and wood branches and started a fire. They prepared some bedding for Dificil, Little Feather and El Vision as other guards and sentries were carefully placed around the perimeter to protect them. Before they settled down to sleep, Dificil told Little Feather of the place he wanted to visit after they rested. He said it was by a clearing in the forests, alongside a creek with clear blue water filled with beautiful exotic fish. "A peaceful place," he said. As Dificil lay down upon a soft cushion of flamingo feathers, he immediately drifted off into a deep sleep. Little Feather could not help but think that it was not just a coincidence that Dificil's shield and his royal family insignia displayed a large jaguar! He looked upon Dificil with awe and pride and shouted out to him, "Teotl! Teotl! Teotl!" (Nahuatl language meaning wonderful, awesome as a god)!

Chapter Twenty
Slumber And
His "Cochitta"

"As Dificil began to sleep, he thought he heard his Nana humming one of her wonderful songs to him even though she wasn't there. He felt at peace and relaxed. He could hear distant waterfalls and the songs of birds too! But all of a sudden, his restful sleep ended, and he began to stir and moan as the same prophetic words rang in his ears!"

With the wind whistling in his hair, he stepped out from his tepee.

The Brisk, fresh air flowed through his nostrils as he smiled, contented to live this great adventure, this life, another day!

As the new sun rose above the horizon, his eyes sparkled and were dazzled by its brightness.

All species of birds, fowl and insects were about him in abundance as he bowed his head to pray, "Oh glorious God of all life, Oh Lord of all being and reason, thank you for another chance to enjoy what you have set before us,

To the four corners of the earth, through the air, over the land and across the sea, I will keep my covenant with you to respect all life, all the animals of whom I will speak, all the plants which I will nurture and cultivate, and all the waterways which will cleanse me, quench my thirst, and carry all sea life for me to eat!

The waves of the precious bison roam the grasslands and make the sounds of thunder upon the earth. I will hunt them for my food, to clothe myself and keep myself warm and shelter my lodge.

Suddenly, alarmingly, "What is that I smell and see? Dark clouds and the scent of death and disease coming from the east!

A horrid, demon-like creature upon a dark horse cometh towards me!"

He carries a sword of pestilence, he brandishes a lance of murder, treachery and deceit, and he spits from his fowl mouth poison upon the crops and fields, as he is a frightening, foreboding creature of no color!

Somehow, he is accompanied by other creatures bearing a Cross!

Who maim, kill and conquer in the name of their god!

They come on large boats that swim through the perilous seas to land and invade us here!

I must hide my spouse and children within the great mountains,

I shall prepare a new, formidable shield to do battle against these coming strange foes!

Or as it was foretold eons ago, that there will be no defense against these cruel intruders, these aliens!

And his company will be as numerous as the filthy, ravenous weeds upon the land!

Dificil then saw "Huitzilopochtli," the Aztec Sun and War God. His eyes fluttered, he struggled to wake himself, and then he saw ……… Mictlantecuhtli"! The god of death! He woke suddenly from this horrid nightmare, sweating profusely as he screamed, No!

No! No! Let this not be our faith! Let this not be our end! Please don't let it be our destiny!

Instantly, Little Feather was standing over Dificil with great fury in his eyes. Llore was growling loudly prone, at his side, ready to pounce, and the great eagle Itta was perched on a tree branch just above him! All the Aguilas were standing alert and ready for any sudden movement by anyone or anything! All the poor little animals and yes, the large ones too, were just standing by, horrified and saddened by the sound of Dificil yelling out! What could be wrong? What is it that is causing Dificil such pain? Who would dare harm the blessed one? Dificil rose to his feet and began rubbing his eyes as he was now fully awake.

"Fear not, for I was just dreaming of my friends. All is well. Let us leave now and continue our journey to another place," Dificil told everyone. Standing just behind him was El Vision. He knew this was the recurring "Cochitta" that Dificil just had, yet he knew somehow something was different this time. As Dificil communicated his dream to El Vision and Little Feather

through their mental telepathy, he described how he saw clearly
the alien foes that would come from another land to try and
destroy their future! Such was the coming invasion! Such was
his vision of an impending horrific annihilation and destruction
of the most glorious legendary civilization, ever known to man!

CHAPTER TWENTY-ONE
"THE BATTLE OF THE CAVES"

"About a half mile north of us is a clearing and a beautiful creek which flows through the woods. Come on, Little Feather, I will show you, and I know you will wonder at the beauty and serenity of this place," exclaimed Dificil. As they traveled along, Dificil pulled wildflowers from the bush to take back to his Mama and to his senior NaNa, and maybe for Consuelo, he thought, smiling as he enjoyed the fresh scents of the flowers and their wonderful colors. He handed them to one of his aides. He and Little Feather were enjoying their excursion through the forest. Without warning, Dificil and Little Feather once again began to run. They moved swiftly to the clearing and the site of the creek. The Aguila escort struggled to keep up with them. As they approached the outside perimeter of the area that Dificil had described, Little Feather's breath was taken away by the sight of such beauty. Multi-colored plants and trees surrounded this clearing, and the soil that they walked on was now much softer and red in color, as he awed at the sight of a large waterfall just in front of them. He could feel the refreshing spray from the waterfall upon his face and the coolness of the earth at his feet!

Among the indigenous tribes, the Indios, there were many stories that waterfalls could be doorways to other worlds, the world of immortals, or the world of the "Little People." There was the sacred ritual of going to the water, as it provides physical and spiritual cleansing prior to ceremonies as well as renewal for daily life, but somehow, at this very moment, Dificil did not feel anything spiritual. Something was not right; something was very strange, and he now sensed alarm and danger!

Little Feather noticed that there were numerous caves now visible along the side of the hill. When first arriving at this site, they did not see the caves because they were hidden by a vast amount of foliage. Dificil did not feel the peace and serenity that he felt the last time he was here, and where were all the wonderful animals? Flying above just ahead of Dificil and his entourage, Itta saw the small opening of a cave. He signaled El Vision that something was amiss. It was not just the scent but his instinct that told him to beware of the presence of something or someone within the caves that were now clearly visible just in front of them! El Vision moved towards Little Feather and he in turn looked directly at Dificil, and everyone suddenly was on guard. Little Feather immediately moved in front of Dificil, poised in his warrior stance as his senses were keenly focused and alert! The Aguila General silently signaled the bodyguards to form themselves in a circle around Dificil. Just then, there was a loud roar and lots of screaming coming from above where the party stood. As if by magic, many little people came into view from inside the hill, into the open and were running down towards Dificil and his companions. Dificil then saw Llore reappear, running after some of the little people. Llore's mouth was covered with blood and what looked like part of a human arm protruding from it! As these cave people approached them, the Aguilas began to repel their attack by thrusting their swords and spears into their bodies. "Atl-tlachinalli!" "Atl-tlachinalli!" the Aguilas repeated over and over! The Azteca War Cry!

The Cave People attacked them with what looked like razor-sharp knives and axes. There seemed to be an endless number of them exiting the caves and attacking. One after another, as the battle was in full swing, the bodies of the cave people began to fall in front of the Aguila circle into a huge pile. The blood flowed, and the screams continued with their deafening sound as the Aguilas repeated their highly trained and skillful thrusting and blocking. Their swords, spears, axes and shields were covered in blood. Somehow, the cave people were able to fight their way through the Aguila wall and got close to Dificil. Little Feather's eyes were dark, lifeless dots of fury. He screamed out as he slashed and hacked at the Cave People. "I will smite all of them, and when I am finished, I will tear off their arms and legs from their bodies. I will disembowel them and tear out their hearts," yelled Little Feather. Suddenly, a spear just missed Dificil's head as it flew by him and struck one of the Aguilas in the back, killing him. Another spear was struck down by Dificil as he swiped it away with his own sword!

More of the Aguilas fell dead or wounded, and it seemed that the cave people were now gaining momentum in this fierce battle! Little Feather was repelling assaults now from every direction. He struggled to stay in front of Dificil, but it was difficult due to the huge number of attackers. Just then, as if he had wings, Dificil leapt above and over everyone and was now behind the diminutives! Dificil was cutting, stabbing, hacking and slashing with both his obsidian sword and dagger! Each powerful stroke took down at least two of the cave people at a time! Through his peripheral vision, he saw the young Aguila that had left headed back to Tenochtitlan. He had been dispatched to acquire reinforcements. Dificil also saw a great pile of bodies strewn to his left and to his right. The blind El Vision displayed his awesome fighting ability. Even though he could not see, he had the miraculous ability to not only block the many blows of the enemy, but he also attacked with great strength and quickness, killing one after another! With his long wooden staff, he struck at the Cave People, crushing their skulls and simultaneously with his sword in his other hand, he decapitated still more!

Each time Dificil smote one of the enemies, his movements seemed to become faster and faster, to the point where his thrusts and slashes were just a blur!

Consuelo was back in Tenochtitlan, asleep when she was suddenly awakened, and screamed, and all present felt a horrible tremor flow through their bodies! At the same time, the Senior NaNa began to scream, the same eerie sound! What was wrong? What was happening? The senior NaNa and the young Amazon Queen yelled at the same time, "Dificil! Dificil! He is in danger; someone is attacking him! Alert the Emperor! Please send help to him!" Consuelo uttered her frantic declaration, and then she yelled out to the senior NaNa, "May the gods get me there in time!" Her Amazon guards followed her as she hurriedly ran towards the forest, directly to the clearing and to the defense of Dificil! The Aguila reinforcements were swift as they followed Consuelo as the Azteca drums pounded louder band louder, with a violent, alarming sound as did the hearts of all the Azteca nation!

At this moment, it appeared as if the whole world was filled with the urgency of the situation! Why, even the heavens were darkened by foreboding, tumultuous clouds!

No one else knew that Dificil had alerted his NaNa and the Amazon through telepathic messages. The emperor had been immediately notified and, along with the Aguilas, rushed towards Dificil! As she ran, Consuelo felt such heaviness in her heart. Tears streamed down her eyes as fear gripped at her throat. Never had she experienced such feelings of alarm and dread! She pushed herself faster and faster. The fear she felt was not for herself but the fear that she would not reach Dificil in time to save him from his enemies. She could not bear the thought of something bad happening to him! She knew if it did, she would die! As she continued to run at such a tremendous speed, sweat ran down her body, and a blazing fever tore at her brain! She did not seem to need to breathe anymore, nor did she care!

Just then, the Aguila, who was dispatched to Tenochtitlan to get help, stopped in his tracks! Yelling out, he said, "Cursed Mictlantecuhtli (the Azteca god of death), it can't be! More attackers are coming from the rear?" As he looked out before him, he saw the huge cloud of dust emanating from the oncoming warriors. As they got nearer to him, he then sighed in relief when he saw the royal banners of the Azteca. He realized that they were not more of the enemy but the Aguila reinforcements, but how did they know? He was the only one sent for help, and he was still en route to alert them, but they were already arriving!

Parts of legs, arms and feet flew! The stench of blood and death was suffocating! With swift movements and cold fury, the Amazon mowed down everything in her path! With eyes ablaze, she tore through the enemy, and many heads began to roll to the ground as she smote the Cave People! She stabbed at their hearts and slashed at them, hacking their bodies to pieces! As she continued to fight her way through the enemy soldiers, she anxiously looked for Dificil! She could now see Little Feather as he too was killing at will and smiting the vermin that dared to attack Dificil. But where was Dificil? Her throat was so dry that she could hardly swallow! As she wiped blood from her eyes, she frantically looked for him! Was he somewhere lying on the ground already dead? Oh no! Oh no! As the reinforcements took over the battle and were killing off the rest of the enemy, Consuelo suddenly saw someone standing under a great pinetree. He was accompanied by a huge white wolf, and a bald eagle sat just above him on a limb, and he was covered from head to foot in blood …………."

"Great Quetzalcoatl! It's Dificil! Praise to all gods, he is alive, he is well, and he is safe," Consuelo screamed to herself as she finally took a breath of air! She rushed towards him! As she did, she saw Little Feather jump in front of him; he too, was covered in blood. She was just steps away from Dificil when Little Feather, recognizing that it was her, stopped cursing and slashing out and then stepped aside. Consuelo dropped both her swords and wrapped her arms around Dificil and sobbed in relief. Dificil was deeply moved by her show of emotion as he squeezed her, and he held her close to him. She looked into his eyes and finally smiled, and then involuntarily kissed him! She immediately stepped back, dropped to her knees and awaited Dificil's next move. He reached down and grabbed her hand, standing her up on her feet as he motioned to the other Amazons to come forward and stand by their Queen. As she stood beside Dificil, she noticed they were now surrounded by hundreds of Aguila. The jubilant warriors were screaming Dificil's name again and again and shouting, "Atl-tlachinalli, Atl-tlachinalli!" the Azteca War Cry, proudly proclaiming their great victory.

Tired and relieved that all the fighting was over, Dificil drank from the flask that was brought to him. The cool water was refreshing and somehow seemed to calm him. As the Aguilas looked on, Dificil's father emerged from the huge group of Aguila reinforcements and happily hugged him saying, "May the gods be offered bountiful sacrifices for us being able to reach you in time! Are you hurt in any way?" he asked. "No Tahtli, I'm not injured, and all the Aguilas fought brilliantly to protect me. Little Feather and Consuelo especially showed their valor and ferocity here today! Many of my Aguila bodyguards have died, and I wish that they be carried back to our city so memorials could be prepared for such brave warriors that they were, and please, Father, may we have the wounded attended to right away," Dificil begged his father. "Pilli," don't worry yourself about the others. All are being cared for as we speak. My own General, El Raton, personally will guard you as you return to Tenochtitlan," he exclaimed. "Tahtli, I do not wish to return to our city with El Raton. As I have told you before, I do not favor such a person in our presence or in our service. I do not like him being close to you in any way!" "Very well, Pilli, we will discuss this further at another time, but for now, please come with me and let us return to the palace so we can cleanse ourselves, rest and be seen by your mother. She anxiously waits for news about you, and I know she will rejoice along with our entire nation when she knows that you are safe." Chichinotpotl was relieved that his son was safe, but at the same time, he knew that he would give the order to put to death the leaders of Dificil's entourage for putting him in harm's way. They had failed in scouting out beforehand the area in which Dificil traveled, and with this failure, put him at risk!

As Dificil stepped away from the battlefield, his very bones shook not just from exhaustion but from the sight of so much blood, death, and terror. Walking alongside his father as they passed by the valiant Aguila warriors who were bathed in blood, Dificil saw the way his father was looking at the Aguilas. His eyes were now filled with rage!

Stopping before Chichinotpotl, Dificil began to speak, "My dear father, I could tell that you are more than disappointed with my bodyguards. I can sense your plans to have them all executed because you feel they have failed in their duty to properly protect me. I know of the strict regimen and edict that you have ordered regarding my care and defense. You can see the many bodies of our Aguilas that lay here because they gave their all to protect me. They all fought so valiantly. I respectfully ask that you open your heart and have mercy on these courageous warriors. Yes, they may have failed in not searching the area where we were attacked beforehand, but death is not a correction of military discipline. If these Aguilas are executed, what will we really gain, and it would be such a terrible, tragic loss! I promise you I will personally see that they are given new, intense, corrective military training of preparedness and scouting procedures."

Placing a hand on his son's shoulder and looking into his eyes, all his eyes, he saw the trauma his son had experienced and the fatigue and sadness. He immediately felt so much compassion for Dificil and acquiesced to his passionate request. "It is true your Aguilas fought valiantly, and so many have already given their lives in your defense."

Because of my love for you and my relief that you survived this attack, I will grant your wish to forgo any punishment of the Aguilas. With a feeling of great relief, Dificil immediately hugged his father and thanked him for his understanding and mercy.

Dificil, and his father, slowly began their triumphant return to Tenochtitlan after such a bloody battle. Llore was walking beside Dificil, also covered with the blood of the Cave People, as he spat out parts of a leg! Itta was flying just above Dificil with blood dripping from his sharp talons. Dificil and his father mounted their royal carryalls as the Aguilas looked on with great love and admiration for him. They had heard his words of concern for the dead and injured Aguilas. They appreciated the "Pilli's" care and attention to their needs before his own! They had fought alongside him and personally witnessed his fury, his valor and great fighting ability, and now his show of love and affection would always be remembered! With great pride and respect, all the Aguilas gave an enthusiastic military salute as Dificil, Chichinotpotl, Little Feather, El Vision and Consuelo passed their formations.

The newest young general named "Moztla," (Tomorrow) pulled El Raton aside and informed him that Chichinotpotl ordered that he walk at the end of the Azteca force. He was told that when he returned to the city, he was to await further orders from him. El Raton looked at this young "upstart" in disbelief. How could he be insulted in such a manner? Why was he excluded from the "inner circle" of the royal entourage? Nonetheless, he of course followed the directive from the young general and awaited the passing of the last of the Aguilas before he too began his journey back to Tenochtitlan.

As he did so, he was already thinking of what plans he must now make to protect his place in the "Royal Order" and what happened that he was suddenly demoted and mistrusted? He must talk to his spies and acquire the knowledge he did not now have as to who was against him. Could someone, somehow, know of his ambitious plans? By the Gods! He suddenly realized he was in much danger! El Raton had come a long way with his career, his life. He had fought many a battle with the enemies of the Azteca. He patiently waited for his "place in the sun," his time when the Gods would smile upon him and, through the great Chichinotpotl, acquire his earned reward to succeed him as the next Tlatoani! Now it seemed all that had changed! Someone had ruined his plans and had stepped in the way! He must quickly smite these enemies, whoever they were! "Whatever it takes, I will succeed, and I really know now the necessity of removing Dificil," he thought to himself.

As El Raton marched towards the city, the great eagle Itta flew overhead, watching him closely!

Chapter Twenty-Two
"A Hero's Triumphant Return"

As Dificil, his father Chichinotpotl and the rest of the entourage entered the great city of Tenochtitlan, they could hear the resounding blare of the conch horns and feel the massive vibrations of the drums as tens of thousands of Azteca citizens came out to greet them! Flowers were laid in their path by the proud citizenry celebrating their great victory. Smoke rose from all the temples where Teopixque were conducting religious ceremonies and offering prayers and sacrifices to the Gods in gratitude for the safe return of Chichinotpotl and the great Dificil! As the people of the Azteca nation turned out to welcome the royal party, the name they yelled out was, Dificil! Dificil! Dificil!

Grateful and relieved with Dificil's return, Consuelo looked at him and Little Feather and saw how they smiled at each other, but with weary eyes. Dificil could not wait to slip into the royal pools and cleanse himself of all the blood and dust and soothe his tired, sore body. As he entered the palace foyer, his Mama and Senior Nana screamed out his name! The Empress Cuicani ran to him and held him in her arms and sighed in relief at the blessing of her son's safe return! She immediately began to examine him from his head all the way down to his 12 toes, of which each one she counted. She just felt that she had to make sure that there was absolutely nothing wrong with her blessed son! "Okay, Mom! Please stop poking me and touching me all over! Everything is there," Dificil exclaimed. The Empress smiled, but with tears still in her eyes as she finished inspecting her baby. "Okay, I will stop my son. I just wanted to make sure that you were not hurt in any way and that all your parts were still there," his Momma said.

Dificil beckoned the Senior Nana to get up from her knees, and she too, was crying as she held Dificil close! As usual, before the NaNas began to attend to Dificil, Consuelo retired to the other chambers. The Nanas removed Dificil and Little Feather's clothes and prepared them for their baths. Entering the pool, Dificil lay back as the Nanas held him up in the water, gently attending to him and washing him. They tenderly rubbed the soft soap into his and Little Feather's bodies. They both now felt so relieved.

Dificil had almost fallen asleep, especially given the wonderful, loving ministrations he was receiving from his Nanas. He opened his eyes, all his eyes as he could see the Empress and the senior Nana still crying. Climbing back out of the hot, volcanic pool, he embraced his mother and the elderly servant, saying, "Mama, Nana, why are you still crying? Are you not glad that I have returned home safely?" he asked. "It is because of our happiness that you were not harmed that we have tears of joy, my dear son," exclaimed his mother. Dificil kissed his Mama and his Nana on the cheek and then ran and dove back into the huge pool. Little Feather followed him, and they began to swim in the volcanic water. They swam back and forth towards both ends of the pool. Spontaneously, two huge, Blue Dolphins appeared and happily shot up into the air from the depths of the pool, enjoying the opportunity to play with Dificil and Little Feather. Everyone present watched happily as they repeatedly shot up to the surface of the water, holding on to the Dolphins. They continued to play for some time and then they exited the pools, allowing the Nanas to dry them and then massage them with warm oils and dress them.

After a while, having returned to the pool area, Consuelo looked at them both. Again, she could not help but be amazed at how they looked so alike! Yes, they looked like twins! She noticed the closeness and the brotherly love they had for each other. She sadly also saw the same weary, traumatized look in their eyes. They had just been through hell and back. Dificil told her he was going to his bedchambers. Consuelo kissed him goodbye and said, "Yes, please go now, my lord and rest. I will see you later, and may the gods provide you with peaceful dreams. They were amorously communicating telepathically also as Little Feather just listened with a bored look on his face."

As they walked through the long corridor Dificil told Little Feather that he was glad that they had been taught at an early age all aspects of martial arts, the use of weaponry, battlefield techniques and physical conditioning. All important tools they used in protecting themselves. It was not only the lessons learned in the Calmecac from the Teopixque, but more so the training they received personally from Chichinotpotl and El Vision. Their ability to survive was the result of their total dedication to that training, and it was worth all the pain and sweat endured during those many lessons!

Dificil was now sitting on a seat made of gold and ivory that was specially made for him. "Come, my son, you should go and sleep for a while, so you will be well rested before the grand dinner that will be held in honor of your great victory," his mother said. "I am weary, mother and I do believe that I need to sleep for a while, even though I know it may be impossible after such a fierce and bloody battle! I feel bad because so many lives were lost. Though those Cave People attacked us and tried to harm us, I am not pleased with the necessity of so much killing and maiming! Despite all the training I received as a warrior, I was not prepared for the experience of seeing so much death," exclaimed Dificil. "My precious son, such are the horrors of war and the taking of life. Neither is pleasant, and only love can heal such trauma," answered his mom.

When Dificil entered his large bedroom, he dove onto his bed and began to fall asleep right away as his Aguila bodyguards stood watch silently, and then he closed his eyes, all his eyes. The Senior Nana sat next to him and reached out to touch his forehead and apply "momotzoa" (Nahuatl language meaning massage).

Then Dificil whispered to his mother, "Cuica! Cuica," (meaning to sing), Dificil's mom's name "Cuicani" derived from the word "Singer." Cuicani was known for her soft but strong, and enchanting voice. She just smiled and, with a heart full of love for her son, began to sing. She began with his favorite song, the same song she had always sung to Dificil since the day he was born. A song their ancestors sang for thousands of years. Magical sounds and expressions filled the air as illustrious tones and healing chants emanated from her voice as she sang the song.

Just Close Your Eyes

Just close your eyes and sleep, my precious Son,

For tomorrow brings new adventures, my Little one.

When you dream, dream of me as I hold your hand,

We will look out from atop the mountain,

Down to the valley, and then out to the open sea.

Soft waves will wash against us as our feet touch the warm sand.

Colorful butterflies fly above you and will nest in your hair,

As the Great Bald Eagles stay perched on the lofty trees,

While the scent of beautiful, fragrant flowers fills the air.

Let the Great Spirit see your happy smile,

And know that my love and my heart will be with you,

All the while!

Dificil again drifted off into a deep sleep with a smile appearing on his face, but then it slowly turned into a dark, sullen frown. Once again, his nightmare began, the "Cochitta," the "Coming!"

With the wind whistling in his hair, he stepped out from his tepee.

The brisk, fresh air flowed through his nostrils as he smiled, contented to live this great adventure, this life, another day!

As the new sun rose above the horizon, his eyes, all his eyes, sparkled and were dazzled by its brightness.

All species of birds, fowl, and insects were about him in abundance as he bowed his head to pray.

"Oh glorious God of all life, oh Lord of all being and reason."

Thank you for another chance to enjoy what you have set before us.

To the four corners of the earth, through the air, over the land and across the sea.

I will keep my covenant with you to respect all life, all the animals of whom I will speak.

All the plants of which I will nurture and cultivate, and all the waterways which will cleanse me, quench my thirst, and carry all sea life for me to eat!

The waves of the precious bison roam the grasslands and make the sounds of thunder upon the earth. I will, with due respect, hunt them for my food, to clothe myself and shelter my lodge.

Suddenly, alarmingly, what's that I smell and see?

Dark clouds and the scent of death and disease coming from the east!

A horrid, demon-like creature upon a dark horse cometh towards me!

He carries a sword of pestilence. He brandishes a lance of murder, treachery and deceit.

And he spits from his foul mouth poison upon the crops and fields,

As he is a frightening, foreboding creature of no color!

Somehow, he is accompanied by other creatures bearing a Cross!

Who maim, kill and conquer in the name of their god!

They come on large boats that swim through the perilous seas to land and invade us here!

I must hide my spouse and children within the great mountains

I shall prepare a new, formidable shield to do battle against these coming strange foes!

Or as it was foretold eons ago.

There will be no defense against these cruel intruders, these aliens!

And their company will be as numerous as the filthy, ravenous weeds upon the land! Dificil had just seen "Huitzilopochtli", the Azteca Sun and War God. His eyes fluttered, He struggled to wake himself, and then he saw………Mictlantecuhtli! The God of Death!

He woke suddenly from his horrid nightmare, sweating profusely, and then he screamed out loud, "No! No! No! Let this not be our faith! Let this not be our end! Please don't let it be our destiny!"

Everyone jumped to attention and on guard as Little Feather was instantly in front of Dificil, ready to strike down anyone or anything that moved towards him! Dificil then sat up in his bed and said, "It is alright, everyone. I was just dreaming. Please stand down and relax!" The alarmed guards, Llore and the eagle Itta, all went back to their respective positions. As Little Feather moved aside for the NaNa, the fury and coldness left his eyes, and he just stood still, with his breathing turning to normal again.

The NaNa stood up and put her arms around Dificil and said, "My dear Dificil, though I only know what I hear from you during your dreams, I can tell they are frightful and foreboding! Fear not, for I have faith that you will prevent this forecast of death and extinction!" The Nana continued to apply "momotzoa," as Dificil again closed his eyes, all his eyes and was finally able to go back to sleep, a more restful sleep without any more horrid nightmares.

It was early evening when Dificil awoke from his nap and strode out to the pool area. He just stood there and looked at his reflection in the water while in deep thought. Having walked up next to him, Little Feather asked, "What is it that causes you to have such horrible dreams as you did this evening, Dificil?" "The dream that I have is a recurring nightmare. I do believe it is a premonition, a warning of what is to come in the future. Each time I have the dream, it seems clearer and clearer to me about what we must do to prepare for this great battle, to prevent our people's annihilation and to save our land. I feel I must meet again with the Tlamatini and all the rest of the Teopixque to describe my nightmare to them and discuss it further. I know that there have been stories written in the past of others describing such visions and foreboding dreams, but none as real or as vivid as mine!" Dificil answered. "You are right to look upon this vision as something real Dificil, not just a bad dream," exclaimed El Vision as he too entered the conversation. What you have seen is a true "Holocaust," the possible end to our world, our way of being and our civilization!

You are the chosen one, your birth and coming of age is a blessing upon this entire world! Most people do not realize it now, but very soon the prophecies of old will take place. They will happen because of your existence and the missions you will complete! I must remind you that there is danger all around us, and you must always be alert and ready. Little Feather will serve you with all his training, skills and wisdom and with all his heart! You must also be receptive to the Amazon Queen, for she too has a purpose, and that purpose is to serve and protect you. And now I know that you have received a telepathic message from the young lady, La Salvadera. We should meet with her after dinner, for she has much to tell. It was such a wise decision and great foresight that you and your father demonstrated in having commissioned this young lady to serve as our eyes and ears! She has learned of El Raton's evil plans and those of the other Aguilas that serve under his command as well. He is much too ambitious and such an evil traitor. He is especially envious of you and your power. If I may say so Dificil, what my eyes cannot see, my ears have heard, and my inner sense tells me a coup is being planned not only to replace your great father, but to eliminate you as the rightful heir to the Azteca crown! Together, we must prepare to meet this great challenge and save the future of the Azteca nation! It's so fortunate that all this time La Salvadera has monitored El Raton's movements. She knows of his meetings and secret excursions away from the city. She has thus been able to listen to his devilish plans and identify his evil cohorts! How convenient, El Raton must have thought, to meet and scheme with our enemies and then return to our domain! Well, now we shall watch him squirm, as his devious plans to betray us fail," El Vision concluded.

"I know all these unfortunate things that you are telling me are true. They are parts of the many pieces of such an evil puzzle that El Raton has devised. I appreciate even more now the many hours I've spent reviewing and studying the history of wars and conflicts past, and hearing of different strategies and mistakes made. We have learned much from you and my father. I can tell you now El Vision, that I have already made some plans on how to deal with this treachery, but of course I appreciate and need your counsel and that of my father's," Dificil exclaimed. El Vision and Little Feather were saddened at the dark and sullen look upon Dificil's face as he walked away. Dificil just shook his head in disbelief at how evil, wicked, and conniving such a person as El Raton could be. After all the years that his father awarded him and provided him with such good fortune, and most of all trusted him, and to think he is supposed to be family! "Know this and remember! In the end, I will reckon with this snake personally!" declared Dificil.

CHAPTER TWENTY-THREE
"SADNESS, REVELATION AND HEALING"

As Dificil reentered his bedroom chamber, he suddenly sensed a great tragedy, a horrible feeling of sadness and the foul scent of death! Just before him, there was someone lying upon the floor! Oh no, it's my Senior NaNa! Dificil ran to her and placed his arm beneath her head as he lifted her slightly so he could look at her face. NaNa! NaNa! What is wrong? What has happened! Please open your eyes! Now that Dificil held her in his arms, he realized that she was near death. She had finally fallen prey to the sickness of her heart that Dificil had diagnosed so long ago, as she first held him when he was born! Dificil remembered he had felt her heavy breathing because her lungs were not working well, and he noticed her irregular heartbeat, her weak pulse. She was so thin and frail, as Dificil diagnosed her terminal illness. Now, as his bodyguards and the other NaNas were around him, Dificil raised his head, closed his eyes, all his eyes and looked into the heavens. Everyone stood silent and still as they suddenly heard a strange, guttural sound emerging from his throat! His chest began to expand and grow larger as he placed his right hand over the forehead of the NaNa! His left hand began to rub her arms up and down. He seemed to be massaging her very veins, and then suddenly, with both his hands clenched in a fist, he pounded her chest over and over again! Another strange and powerful sound which seemed to come from his very soul rang out again! With one hand, he squeezed her forehead, and with the other, he continued to massage her arms! An intense look was upon his face. A bright light began to emanate from the area of the NaNa's head, which was covered by Dificil's hand! Everyone stared in shock and disbelief! Then everyone dropped to their knees before Dificil and bowed their heads to the ground! Minutes had passed, which seemed like hours, and now everyone felt the movement of Dificil and saw the NaNa rising from the floor! Dificil told everyone to rise also and exclaimed, "Do not fear! All is well and my NaNa is healed!" Everyone looked up from the floor, and they couldn't believe their eyes! There she was, as if nothing had happened to her! The Senior NaNa was now standing on her own power and smiling at her beloved Dificil! As he continued to hold her and look into her eyes, he saw confusion and wonderment! She knew Dificil had brought her back from the throes of death, but she did not know how. This was one of the rare times that Dificil demonstrated his healing powers. Somehow, he had healed her and kept that most evil, terrible demon death from taking her!

Dificil looked at her and smiled through the tears that still filled his eyes. "Go now, my NaNa. Go now and rest and tell no one of what has happened here today. Everyone listen! This is not something that should be described or revealed to anyone outside this circle! They again bowed their heads in obedience and gasped in wonderment at what to them surely was a miracle! They all knew the NaNa was very ill for a long time, and her condition worsened as each day passed. No one had expected her to survive for much longer, and when she lay upon the floor dying, somehow Dificil had revived her! He saved her! He cured her and defied death!"

Dificil then stepped out into the corridor just outside his bed chambers. He was happy that through the blessings of the Great Creator, he was able to save his beloved Senior Nana, but his heart and his mind could not help but still be heavily affected by all that happened because of the battle with the Cave People. As he had told his mother and his NaNa upon returning from the battlefield, it was very hard for him to accept so much death, so much killing and maiming! Just then, many dark clouds appeared in the sky! Large balls of hail began to rain down on the earth as Dificil began to slowly walk back to his private chambers. Dificil touched the head of each Aguila that he passed, and they felt blessed and yet were saddened not only because of the loss of their comrades, but because they saw the great pain and hurt in their Dificil!

Little Feather and El Vision walked alongside him in silence, as did Llore and Itta, who was quietly flying just above him, sensing the troubled sadness of the Pilli.

Chapter Twenty-Four
"Regret, Remorse and Forgiveness"

The whole of Tenochtitlan was quiet and subdued. The great city seemed almost lifeless! The sky was still dark, and the rain and hail had stopped, but the wind was still blowing hard and chilled a body to the bone! There seemed to be a profound sadness in the air. It seemed to be as if the sky itself echoed the sounds of despair! Animals didn't stir. Birds stayed perched in their trees and did not fly, and if one looked upon the waterways, it seemed as if the fish just floated in stillness. Every living creature of the kingdom knew that all was not well for the great Dificil.

Dificl stood next to his bed with his arms at his side. He was motionless, barely breathing as he went into what seemed to be a trance. Unbeknownst to everyone, he was in a deep state of meditation. El Vision and Little Feather were standing next to him, and everyone else present just stood by and watched worriedly. El Vision then seemingly relaxed with a smile on his face as he sat down. He was the only one present who knew.

Dificil was in spiritual, concentration, connecting to the Great Creator and with all the spirits past!

Little Feather had immediately dropped to his knees in front of Dificil and screamed out pleading to him, "My dear brother, please open your eyes. Speak to me and tell me you are alright!" Somehow, out of nowhere came the Amazon, Consuelo. She too, knelt next to Dificil. She had started to feel his pain and sadness when he first arrived in his bed chambers, and she knew something was terribly wrong! She had run from her own room to find out what was causing Dificil such stress and suffering. Now Chichinotpotl was very frightened at what seemed like a sudden illness of his son. He immediately ordered the Tlamatini to begin making sacrifices to the gods and to pray for Dificil's recovery. El Vision could feel Chichinotpotl's stress and worry. He got up and walked over to his Emperor and softly told him not to worry, that Dificil was just conducting a spiritual communication with their Great Creator.

As he continued to be still and silent, his mother, Chichinotpotl, his Senior NaNa and Consuelo, all sat solemnly at the foot of his bed. One could see the worried look upon the face and the eyes of even Llore and Itta as the Teopixque continued to chant prayers and words of lamentations to the gods! Large candles were all around Dificil's bed as incense continued to burn and fill the air around the chambers. The Teopixque now dropped to their knees, and their bodies were shaking as they noticed a strange aura all around Dificil. A soft, slow, steady beat of drums could be heard from outside as the Azteca nation was at an eerie standstill!

In his deep trance, Dificil looked out upon "Anahuac" (The Valley of Mexico). "Am I dreaming? Is this for real? Why does it seem as if there is no sound, no wind, nothing moving? Aye, here, just before the horizon is this "Aztlan," (Paradise)! I feel like I must rest. I must close my eyes and replenish my energy. Oh, Aztlan, how beautiful, all the pyramids, such splendid architecture, statues and beautiful paintings! Is this just "Machitil" (Nahuatl word meaning a sign)?" Suddenly standing before him was the great chieftain, "Tenoch," the first great ruler, "Tlatoani" of Tenochtitlan! He appeared before Dificil surrounded by a host of large clouds and lightning.

"Look Dificil. Look out as far as you can see! This is your land! This will be your rightful prize as the future Tlatoani of Tenochtitlan and the Aztec nation." Somehow Dificil knew he sat atop the "Great Pyramid," the Huitzilopochtli's shrine. This, as all previous Tlatoani before him had done, was the ritual to his coronation and his becoming king of the Azteca nation! Tenoch presented him with a jaguar's claw for sacrificial bloodletting from his ears and legs. Upon his head was placed the crown of green stones, all worked in gold along with many other decorative adornments upon his body and head. He was taken by the hand to a throne that was called the "Cuauhicpalli" meaning eagle-seat, also named jaguar seat, for it was decorated with eagle feathers and jaguar hides. Dificil looked out upon the wide expanse of land. As far as he could see there were his people and a countless number of other calpolli. He could see all the animals of the earth and great waterways leading up to his beloved Tenochtitlan. He saw many great armies of Toltecs, his ancestors and other Aguilas looking up towards him at the crest of the Great Pyramid but he also saw dismay, fear and horror in their eyes! Now he could see that the Toltecs and Aguilas stood in pools of blood and tears! "What does this mean? What does this vision convey?" yelled out Dificil. He noticed something else strange as he continued to look out on his land. There was somehow a feeling of emptiness, a sad feeling of loss and death! He reached out with his arms to the left; he reached out with his arms to the right, behind him and in front of him! "Where is Little Feather? Where has he gone? Has something happened to him? This can't be, and yet even in this traumatic spiritual-like experience, Dificil sensed hope and encouragement! He felt the beckoning of his forefathers to complete his historic mission! "What's that I see, three giant men?"

No, three nations. They are motioning for me to help them come together! He thought again, "What does this mean?" he yelled out loud from his deep state of meditation! Feverish and sweating profusely, Dificil suddenly returned to normal, and everyone present screamed! They didn't scream in fear but in relief that their beloved Dificil finally returned from his death-like stillness. As the priest-physicians began to examine him, Dificil suddenly yelled out, "Stop! Stop! What are you doing! I am not even hurt! I didn't go anywhere! I'm still here! They couldn't find anything physically wrong with him, other than a slight fever. As they checked his eyes, all his eyes, his breathing, the beats of his heart and the pulse of his blood vessels, he seemed to be well! Chichinotpotl ordered everyone to leave the room but his mother, his Senior NaNa, Consuelo, Little Feather, and El Vision. Llore and the Itta still cautiously stood guard by the door."

"My precious son, are you now well? Has the evil spirit left your soul and released you back to me," asked the Empress Cuicani as she continued to rub the soft, cool cloth over Dificil's forehead. Cuicani remembered how, after first meeting Consuelo, Dificil seemed to be bewitched, but now he was totally different! She had never seen anything so strange in her lifetime!

Kneeling at his side, both his Senior NaNa and Consuelo each held one of his hands and, through tears of joy, smiled at him relieved! "I feel better, mother and father, and now I feel a great need to again, to return to the pools and bathe and cleanse myself from the sweat of these strange visions that I have just experienced. I must speak with you, my father, El Vision and the great Teopixque as we together can determine what the full message is that I have received today of our future and the missions that have been put before me," Dificil exclaimed. The great Chichinotpotl just nodded yes in his response. He was spellbound and awed like many times before, since the birth of Dificil. This creature before him, his son, was truly, "The Chosen One!" He felt that he really was a gift of the gods, a real descendant of Quezaltcoatl!

Returning to the volcanic pools, Dificil finished his bath and allowed the Nanas to apply the comforting oils and soothing lotions upon him. Little Feather just watched in silence. Dificil had swam so many times before with the Dolphins, but at this moment, he did not want to. His mind seemed to be off unto some distant place.

Just then, El Vision stood next to his son, Little Feather. "I could feel the sadness in your heart, but don't worry, my son." What you see and feel of Dificil is only natural. Dificil is now really within his realm of greatness. First, he experiences his

Cochitta, then his visions through his spiritual mediation. These incidents aren't strange or surprising to me or the Teopixque for they are realities that were foretold long ago. This is part of Dificil's baptism into the real life of a Tlatoani! Such traumatic experiences and profound incidents are just part of his coming of age. These are things that he, as the future of the Azteca nation, must accept and learn from. Before him lie many great historic times and he must be prepared to understand what happens around him, adjust to it, make decisions and react in a way that will protect his people and pave the way for a bright future for them. The responsibilities and tasks before him are endless," El Vision concluded. He too was filled with such great pride and love for his son Little Feather. He then placed his hand upon his shoulder to comfort him.

As El Vision and Little Feather looked on, Llore the huge wolf, walked up to Dificil and pushed his nose under his arm and purred as he seemed to not only be comforted by Dificil but tried to comfort him! Dificil held Llore close as he ran his hand upon his head over and over again. He told Little Feather that he was feeling better and was ready for what lie ahead. Just then, Dificil rose to his feet and looked directly at Little Feather and El Vision! He again felt a sense of danger and apprehension as he received the telepathic transmission from the eagle. The eagle Itta told him that an emissary had arrived from the Tarascan nation and that he was to be introduced by the villainous general, El Raton. Dificil shook his head from side to side, indicating his displeasure. Little Feather and El Vision had a look of worry, and Llore immediately went into his attack stance! His ears stood straight up, and his huge fangs protruded from his mouth as he growled. They all knew that their enemies were near and poised as vipers to strike at them and the Azteca nation!

Before Dificil, Little Feather and El Vision were fitted with their ceremonious apparel for the great dinner, they smiled at each other for they had also received some good news through an additional telepathic message from the young lady, La Salvadera. She had just arrived with the emissaries of the Tarascan nation. Her message was simple but urgent. She had important, secret information for them. Unbeknownst to anyone else, she was also very anxious to see her beloved Dificil!

Chapter Twenty-Five
"Dinner Preparation and the Meeting"

Elaborate and extensive preparations had been made to have everything perfect for the dinner that was to be held for Dificil to honor him in celebrating his glorious victory in the battle with the Cave People. Within this temple, this special palace, which had been built before the birth of Dificil's grandfather, it was evident how much work and artistry were put into its making. There were long corridors leading to the main chamber and the dining area. Each corridor's walls were decorated in glorious colors and displayed statues and murals of Azteca rulers from the past who were Dificil's ancestors, his lineage. Adjacent to each wall flowed small water canals, filled with exotic fish. Palm trees and many different types of plants and flowers adorned the hallways, such beauty, such splendor! Most of the floral arrangements were of various shades of green to honor Dificil, being that his shield was of the Jaguar, whose insignia always was emblazoned with the color of green. Each table was draped with fine, silk coverings embroidered with pictures of the sun, the moon and with an eagle on a cactus. There were servants specifically assigned for each task. Their expertise illustrated their overflowing pride in their work and their love for Dificil! Small water fountains made of marble and onyx were located at the center of each corridor. Food from throughout the Azteca Empire was brought and prepared for this great feast. Varieties of "tamales" (maize-corn husk), filled with beans, different types of meats, peppers and cheeses were cooked. A wide variety of fish, venison, tender meats of birds from far-off lands, greens and vegetables and fruit of every kind were delivered to the royal palace and prepared. Most of all, the food was brought forth from the Azteca's own Chinampa district, where much of the farming of their Empire was done.

As planned, before the grand dinner, Dificil, his father Chichinotpotl, El Vision, Little Feather, the young General, Moztla and of course, the Amazon Queen all stepped inside a side chamber to talk to La Salvadera.

"The young girl has grown up to be a beautiful woman," exclaimed Dificil as he told La Salvadera to rise to her feet. "It has been many moons since the last time we communicated, my dear friend. I pray that you are well and look forward to us spending some time together," Dificil concluded. Everyone present suddenly looked around as they heard what seemed to be the sound of an animal growl, but it was just an angry, involuntary grunt that came from the Amazon Queen. Already quite attached to Dificil, she didn't appreciate or like the presence of another woman with him, especially when she heard his fond words directed to this stranger. Dificil reached over and affectionately rubbed his hand on the Amazon's back and smiled at her to calm her down as he introduced her to La Salvadera. "La Salvadera is a very close friend of my family. Her lifelong mission is to be our eyes and ears throughout many different parts of our empire. She has the unique talent of speaking in many different tongues, and she is also very persuasive in her conversations," Dificil explained to the Amazon queen. La Salvadera, this is Consuelo. She's the Amazon Queen who was brought up from the southernmost part of our region. She's very close to me personally and has distinguished herself in her efforts to protect me, and she's also one of my very close confidants. She's the ruler of her own people of the Amazon and has pledged to form an alliance with the Azteca, and I must confess that she has taken a special place within my heart, and I hold her dear to me, concluded Dificil.

Upon hearing this revelation from Dificil, Consuelo's face brightened and beamed with pride and joy. It softened somewhat the ferocious dark frown that initially appeared upon her face as she took the hand of La Salvadera. "I have already heard of your awesome combatant qualities Consuelo. You needn't disturb yourself about my intentions, for I'm not here to challenge you or cause a demonstration of your ferocity. I say that because of the ravenous picture that appeared in your eyes upon my arrival. I feel that yours is a true and understandable jealous reaction to any other female in the presence of Dificil. I wish to further state that both our goals and tasks in life are the same, to serve and protect Dificil and the Azteca Kingdom," La Salvadera concluded. As she finished her exchange with Consuelo she stared coldly into her eyes. "It is true La Salvadera, we both have a mutual responsibility. We will both do whatever is necessary to protect Dificil from any harm or danger and of course, ensure the preservation of the Azteca kingdom. I trust you will demonstrate your loyalty and dedication to Dificil here today with your revelations concerning the plans of the Tarascans and advise us on how best to defeat the treachery that they have presented. I too am earnestly watching and listening to everything and everyone at this most precarious time and will most assuredly cut the heart out of any person or thing that comes close to Dificil! So, there is no need to further discuss either of our intentions because we must focus on a strategy of how we may meet this challenge before us," concluded Consuelo. She couldn't help but notice the look of great affection that was visible in the eyes of La Salvadera when she looked upon Dificil. Though it was midday, and the temperature was supposed to be very hot surrounding them, everyone suddenly felt the cold air that filled the room in the presence of these two young women!

Chichinotpotl couldn't help but smile after hearing the incredulous exchange between Consuelo and La Salvadera. This was another of the many fantastic facts that he witnessed many times before. Most women seemed to be mesmerized by Dificil and were enraptured by him!

"Let us all lend our full attention to La Salvadera now and allow her to report on what these conspirators have planned for us," exclaimed the emperor! La Salvadera began her report, "Like us, the Tarascans have spies too. They quickly learned of Dificil's fighting ability and the victory of the battle with the Cave People. Many times, I have been summoned to sit in on meetings of the Tarascans with different people so I could serve as their translator. As you know, my emperor, I have previously sent you information about the dealings and treachery of the Tarascans."

Upon hearing their evil plans sometimes, it has been very difficult for me just to sit still and listen. I have often wanted to strike out and smite them. Now their most wicked plot ever involves Dificil, and their plan to assassinate him! The Tarascans believe that they must make a move on our kingdom now, for they fear that if they wait any longer, Dificil will become stronger and stronger, and then they will never be able to defeat us. This is a revelation from their leader himself. Upon receiving information about Dificil since his birth, the Tarascans know of his greatness, his power and his apparent anointment by the Gods themselves! They have been communicating to other Capolli their plans of attacking us and trying to overthrow our kingdom. As all present listened intently, La Salvadera continued with her most important information, including that of crucial maps that she had made of strategic defensive placements of the Tarascans. As she spoke, she forced herself not to look into Dificil's eyes, all his eyes, for when she did, she felt that she would just melt, fall and die with a smile on her face! Such was the effect Dificil had on her. La Salvadera stated that the Tarascans had met numerous times with "El Raton," who proved to be a traitor and most envious conspirator. In many of his conversations with the Tarascan leadership, he talked of his contempt for Dificil and his anger with Chichinotpotl, especially since he had been separated from the emperor's "inner circle."

El Raton was told by the Tarascan Chieftan that he could obtain the position of "Tlatoani" of the Azteca, after helping them eliminate Chichinotpotl and Dificil. Their plan was simple. At the dinner this evening, they will invite Dificil to go meet the Tarascan emperor's daughter in their city. Dificil would be receiving a hero's welcome, and the Tarascans would make a real show of honoring him and celebrating with him. At this time, the Tarascan emperor would also offer the hand in marriage of his daughter, "Fea", so as to supposedly unify both kingdoms by this marriage and create an alliance. Dificil and Chichinotpotl would be brought to the center of the city during the celebration, and in front of everyone, they would both be assassinated! This horrible deed would be done by "El Raton" himself! In the meantime, 1,000 Tarascans, 10,000 Psuites, and 5,000 Huexotzingans would be standing by at the perimeter of Tenochtitlan, waiting to launch a surprise attack and then go on and plunder the Azteca Empire!

La Salvadera could not help herself, as she was finishing with her report of the planned demise of Dificil and Chichinotpotl, she ran up to Dificil, held him tightly and began to cry and scream out! Consuelo immediately drew her sword from its sheath and charged at her. Dificil quickly put out his arm and told her to stay back. He told her that La Salvadera meant him no harm and that she was just expressing her deep concern and care for his safety. As La Salvadera regained her composure, Little Feather too, was still fuming at this revelation and involuntarily was uttering profanities! Such evil treachery! "Such a devilish, foul traitor El Raton turned out to be," he yelled. An air of tenseness and rage filled the room. The Tlamatini began singing a prayer and waved a canister of incense in the air. Suddenly, a strange smile appeared on Dificil's face! A smile that didn't reflect happiness but just sheer rage and a foreboding sign of danger! The Tlamatini dropped to his knees and began to wail! Everyone else just stood frozen and stared at

Dificil. It seemed as if an animal-like spirit overtook him! His face was now dark, and his eyes, all his eyes, were coals of fire! The Tlamatini again was chanting and praying, as everyone else remained silent! Even Llore dropped to his knees and moaned and howled! Dificil raised his fist to the sky and uttered some very strange words in an unknown language. Now out of fear everyone was on their knees too, only Chichinotpotl stood still and then walked over to his son, placed his hand upon his forehead and said, "What is this spirit that has taken over my son? What foreboding signs are imminent that my son is overtaken by such fury and melancholy," asked the emperor.

The cold icy smile disappeared from Dificil's face but in its place a dark, solemn look was now evident as he spoke, "It's sad that so much blood will be shed again! Many good warriors' bodies will be torn apart, heads will roll, and many will die, all but just for a few envious and greedy people," exclaimed Dificil. The elderly Tlamatini then raised both his hands above his head and asked Dificil for permission to speak. "Speak up, my great learned teacher! Continue with your words of wisdom!"

"My lords, I beseech you to not fall prey to anger and haste, but to maintain full control and implement all your powers and strengths to prepare for this situation. You must know that the enemy has been patiently planning this move for many moons. Ah, yes, El Raton has provided them with much information as to our military might, our city fortifications and our causeway system. The traitor has given them what he thinks is the formula to not only destroy you and your father but our whole empire! I would most sincerely advise that we all enter the dinner calm and relaxed. We must smile, be cordial and appear to receive these emissaries as friends and allies. We must not alert them in any way that we are aware of their treachery. You must receive the Tarascan emperor's daughter warmly and with respect. The gods are busy this evening watching my lord Chichinotpotl and you Dificil. They are expecting to see you both fulfill their prophecies and defend the Azteca. You must show your intelligence, cunning and bravery, and you must also have a strong heart. You must demonstrate your ability to lead, and you must come down hard on your enemies and annihilate them with no mercy! You should also listen closely to General Moztla, though he is young in his age he is experienced traveling to these different lands. He knows these Tarascan devils well and he can advise you on how best to defeat them! Shaking with fear because he spoke so boldly to the "Pipiltin" (nobles), the Tlamatini concluded," I hope my words do not offend you my lords, but with such apparent danger that has presented itself, I feel most obligated to tell you the truth and not make anything seem less precarious than it really is!" "Your counsel is most valued, my dear priest. Now let us all hear what you suggest as the best strategy, General Moztla, so that we shall know our enemy and can be fully armed and ready for this Tarascan battle," Chicihnotpotl commanded.

General Moztla began, "The Tarascans know how important the 'Triple Alliance' is to us and how thus we will be able to increase, strengthen and stabilize our power. Therefore, they chose this time to try to overthrow us before we make that alliance permanent. They have recruited other calpolli who are also our enemies, so.................."

Chapter Twenty-Six
"The Lair of a Warrior and Preparations for War"

General Moztla felt almost hypnotized after being stared at by Dificil. It was his eyes, all his eyes that were so powerful and seemed to be able to look right through you, but as the general also looked at Little Feather standing next to Dificil, he as many times before, noticed something else. Something that caused a sudden, brilliant flash of an idea!! Standing alongside each other, Dificil and Little Feather looked as "Coatl"! (The Nahuatl word meaning serpent or twin). The General thought to himself, "If I didn't know any better, upon looking at both young men, I would think they were identical twins! There seems to be nothing that is different in any way about their features, their height, their weight or the way they walk. Only if one got up close enough to see Dificil's eyes could they notice a difference in the two of them?"

Loud thunder rumbled in the sky! Large black clouds flew high overhead, and there was an eerie silence that blanketed the horizon. Azteca warriors, young and old, held their wives close to them and played with their children because they were aware that this could very well be their last night to enjoy such happiness and comfort. Each warrior knew that when they went to war, there was a good chance that they very likely would not return, and yet they looked forward to the forthcoming battle. This is what they were trained for and what they lived for, especially for the honor to defend the emperor Chichinotpotl and the great Dificil! The "Frontline Warriors" prepared their weapons, sharpening, cleaning and inspecting every single object, every warrior's tool. Many had fought before and experienced the horrors of war, the fighting and butchery that came with being chosen to be the first to attack on the frontline in mortal combat and death!

The powerful scent of incense permeated the thick summer air. Soft fires burned in the still of the night from atop each pyramid temple. The Teopixque presented offerings and prayers to the Gods in preparation for war and blessings upon the Azteca fighting men. Word had been spread quickly and quietly to the Aguila about their secret mission. They would be moving the next night after the scouts had been dispatched ahead of them, as silently as possible through the mountains towards the Tarascan city, separate from the royal entourage, which would leave the next day. As their orders received indicated, they would be led by Gen. Moztla and El Vision. All the warriors from within Tenochtitlan and the outlying areas knew this was a special mission because it had been many, many moons since they were required to travel at night, especially through the mountains, where even most mountain goats had difficulty walking. After so many years of practicing the art of "Ando Ciego" (the Blind Walk); now most assuredly the Aguilas realized the great importance and value of this learned skill!

Dificil appeared to be looking directly at Little Feather, but his eyes seemed to be focused somewhere else. Noticing this, Little Feather approached him and asked, "What's wrong Dificil? I can see that there is something else troubling you. "I don't know my dear brother," but I fear there is something right in front of us, something we cannot see, something that's just not right. I know everyone has carefully planned this whole mission down to every detail, but I still can't help but feel a foreboding sign," Dificil exclaimed. "Don't worry, I will protect you all the way Dificil," Little Feather said. "Oh yes, I am quite confident of that, my dear brother, but it is you that I am worried about," he answered.

Chapter Twenty-Seven
"A Stately Dinner and a Watchful Eye"

Consuelo hummed a soft tune as she was being attended to by the young Nanas. She was nervous. She wondered how everyone would react to her when she was seen in the company of Dificil and the royal family. She was sure that it would be a shock to many, for she knew that word had spread around since her arrival in Tenochtitlan that she had become part of the royal family. After bathing, she was dressed in the finest apparel, and she wore beautiful, sparkling jewelry and golden adornments in her luxurious, long hair. As she walked towards the door of her bed chamber, her Amazon bodyguards smiled with happiness at the sight of how beautiful she was! Even the Senior NaNa gasped in awe at her beauty. Just then, El Vision walked up next to her and asked the Amazon queen to join him and step outside into the corridor, where Dificil was waiting for her. Consuelo placed her hand upon the outstretched arm that was offered to her by El Vision. As she followed him into the corridor, Dificil looked upon her in astonishment and said, "You are such a lovely creature, and you take my breath away!" Before she began to kneel, Dificil grabbed her arm and told her to walk alongside him.

Little Feather then repositioned himself, following close behind. Walking towards the dining chamber, Consuelo could see the great Chichinotpotl and the Empress Cuicani waiting for them at the entrance doors. As they arrived in front of the Emperor and Empress, the Amazon Queen, along with everyone else, stopped and immediately went to their knees with their heads bowed in respect. Again, Dificil took Consuelo's arm and bid her to rise. As the Empress acknowledged Consuelo she began to say, "In the short time that you have been with us, my dear young lady, your combative exploits have already become legend. Having the opportunity to see you formally dressed for our special dinner, I now know that your beauty will also become legendary! It's simple to see why my son is so mesmerized and taken by your companionship!" "My dear Empress, your words of praise are too kind! I feel as if I am in a dream to be privileged to be in your company and to be welcomed by you and your family! You must know that it is now my lifelong blessing and mission to always stand at his side and protect him," Consuelo answered.

The huge golden doors opened, and a blast from the royal horns cascaded from wall to wall throughout the dining chamber as the royal family entered. In the foreground, Azteca warriors and some of the other Teopixque began a dance in their honor. Some of the dancers were dressed in full military dress with their beautiful shields and banners. They were of the 'Otontin (Otomies) and the "Cuauhchique" "Shorn Ones" military Societies. These were the two highest military orders of the Azteca. Both the Eagle and Jaguar were displayed by these two societies. They were also the personal bodyguards of Dificil. As the royal family continued into the room, resounding, beautiful music filled the air. Harps, flutes, drums, and conch horns could be heard as they were performed by the finest musicians in all Tenochtitlan.

The rulers of each of the two other nations, part of the Triple Alliance, were all present and brought with them many rich gifts and exotic food and fruit from their lands. All heads continued to be bowed until the royal family was seated at their table. As Dificil sat, Llore immediately positioned himself at his feet under the table. Dificil, Little Feather and Consuelo couldn't help but laugh at the startled looks they saw on the faces of some of the guests. Many people had never seen a wolf as huge in size as Llore. He could barely fit his big body under the table! As always, the eagle Itta was perched just above Dificil on one of the huge rafters of the roof, closely watching everyone. All eyes were on the royal family. Such a majestic view! All the exhaustive preparations that were performed were successful in providing such an elegant, festive and glorious atmosphere. Invited guests from other subservient provinces were awed at such splendor and richness exhibited by the Azteca!

Though she understood the strategy, Consuelo could not help but be disappointed that she couldn't sit next to Dificil. Yes, she had been present at the meeting that took place prior to the dinner and knew of the careful plans made by General Moztla on behalf of Dificil and the Emperor Chichinotpotl, but she still was not happy. General El Raton was allowed to participate in the ceremonious dinner. He took it upon himself to introduce the Tarascan family to the Azteca royalty. As he did so, every one of the Azteca smiled and tried to show congeniality in place of contempt and hatred. This is what the Tlamatini and General Moztla had prescribed as the best behavior to conceal their knowledge of all the evil and treachery planned by El Raton and the Tarascans. Pleasantries were exchanged as all the introductions were conducted. The Tarascans made a formal invitation to Chichinotpotl and Dificil to come to their capital city as honored guests. They also stated that they wanted to form an alliance with the Azteca. The Tarascan emperor announced that he wanted to offer his daughter in marriage to Dificil as a means of certifying this alliance.

Listening to this conversation, Consuelo, seated just a few feet away, momentarily appeared to be having a seizure or some kind of overt reaction as she was beside herself trying to control her anger. She wished she could kill the vermin right there and then! The Tarascan Emperor, Empress and their daughter were seated just across from Dificil. Consuelo was fuming at the sight of her young daughter as she was conversing with Dificil. She couldn't stand the thought of the demon's ugly daughter getting anywhere near her Dificil! She went to great lengths to keep her composure and not leap at the Tarascan princess and cut her heart out! She almost vomited when she heard the Tarascan offer his daughter in marriage to Dificil. At that very moment, she noticed the smile on Dificil's face as he looked at her and, through their mental telepathy, told her to be calm and pay no heed to such idiocy! Consuelo inspected this female enemy and observed how skinny she was! Her body looked to be that of a young boy. Her hair was very thin without a wave, and she seemed to be going bald! She was so shapeless, and she looked as if she had no breasts whatsoever! After hearing her name,

Consuelo thought to herself, "Fea, such a befitting name for such a horrible looking monster! In the Nahautl language, Fea meant "ugly!"

The friends of the Azteca, who were also members of the Triple Alliance, the rulers of Tlacopan and Tetzcoco, were astounded by the presence of the Tarascans. Wisely, they had been warned beforehand by El Vision to just go along with the charade and act as if they knew nothing. Indeed, this was difficult for them for they too hated the treasonous Tarascans, and they knew that in the very near future they would be at war with these same people! The Tarascans in turn, were not pleased by seeing the Tlacopan and Tetzcoco emissaries there either.

Strategic precautions had been taken to keep them separated throughout the evening. As the festivities continued, the Tarascans seemed to be enjoying themselves greatly.

Chichinotpotl noticed the grotesque eating habits of the Tarascans. They seemed to eat constantly throughout the evening as if they were starving. The Tarascan leader and his spouse were both rotund and obscenely ill-mannered. El Raton was allowed to sit in the company of the two royal families. He somehow felt a renewed confidence during these festivities and glowed as he acted as a negotiator between the Azteca and the Tarascans. He even felt a little remorse as he thought of the result of all these theatrics! Too bad, he really did enjoy all his years serving under Chichinotpotl, but ever since the birth of Dificil, all his plans and aspirations seemed to end abruptly! He thought that surely his emperor cousin should have shown him more respect and gratitude! El Raton seized upon an opportunity to speak directly to Chichinotpotl, "My dear Emperor, I would earnestly recommend that you consent to an alliance with these Tarascan friends. This joining will strengthen our people and bring about more wealth and territories to our kingdom. The Tarascan emperor has mentioned to me many times in the past how he wished to unite the Tarascan nation with the Azteca. It is to my great delight that we finally have come to the threshold of such an alliance!"

Chichinotpotl could not help himself as he responded, "My most trusted cousin, am I to understand that it was your idea to arrange this alliance? You have invested much effort in such an important union. It is amazing how you could conserve so much time to meet with the Tarascan emperor on many occasions and still have time to direct my armies and serve our people!" All of a sudden, El Raton felt a cold chill run through his body because what the emperor expressed to him was not really words of praise but words of rebuke and distrust! He became very wary and subdued. He immediately moved away and sat alone from where the nobles were. Chichinotpotl noticing this called out to him, "General, please come and sit next to me and join us in celebrating such great plans of our future. I must say that I will justly award you for such hard work and dedication to duty!"

Chapter Twenty-Eight
"War, Annihilation and Azteca Supremacy"

A portion of the battlefield veterans, the "Otonies" and the "Cuahchique", the most elite Aguilas, were left behind to protect Tenochtitlan and their people. All the Azteca warriors took part in the ritual sacred rites of animal sacrifices, prayers and fasting during the week before their planned battle. As was the custom before a war, paper flags were placed on fruit trees and houses, but because of the secrecy of this mission, this ritual was not conducted. The Teopixque dressed as deities and danced before the pyramid fires, as did Chichinotpotl and Dificil, another of the ceremonial preparations for war.

On the morning of the battle, facing the Pipiltin (royals), the Tlamatini had incense and candles burning all around them. He began the ceremony of seeking blessings and protection for them all. He was joined by other high priests, "Mexicatl Teohuatzin, (the overseer of ritual), the "Huitznahua Teohuatzin" and "Tecpan Teohuatzin", who governed the rest of the priestly orders. Among them were some of the warrior-priests who carried effigies of deities in the front of all the army. With his arms raised towards the sun and with his smoke pipe held in his right hand, the Tlamatini began his prayer, "To the four winds shall our sacred 'popoca' (smoke) fill the skies. Let there be good 'pahtlli," (good medicine) for our beloved Azteca. Protect them and let not an enemy spear or arrow pierce them." As the great Chichinotpotl and his son Dificil are "Teotl" (something sacred, as gods), please reward them a total victory," concluded the Tlamatini. This ceremony was conducted prior to them leaving Tenochtitlan, as many other prayers and lamentations to the war god Tlaloc were made.

El Raton was engulfed in his own false sense of triumph and mockery of the Azteca royalty. On the night of the great dinner meeting, he let himself get totally drunk, and he stood that way throughout the week before the planned meeting with the Tarascans. Unaware of the plans of Chichinotpotl and Dificil, he had let his guard down and did not detect anything amiss. Slow to wake the day of their departure for the Tarascan city, El Raton got ready. He was shocked when he learned that he was reinstated as the Supreme Azteca General and would lead Dificil and his Aguila escort on such an important mission!

Though nervous and somewhat apprehensive, General Raton's face beamed with pride as he led the royal entourage into the Tarascan capitol city, Tzintzuntzan. He and his Aguila commanders were greeted by the Tarascan Emperor and Empress and their royal entourage. Conch seashell horns blared, and the royal palanquin was softly placed upon the ground by the bearers to allow, who they thought was, the great Dificil to step out and meet the Tarascan officials. Chichinotpotl had advised the Tarascans prior to this date that he wouldn't be able to participate because this event was the same day the Azteca celebrated the feast of the "Tecuilhuitontli, "The Feast of the

Lords." As Tlatoani of the Azteca, he was required to preside over the holy festival. None were aware that Chichinotpotl was secretly poised to attack with his son Dificil, along with El Vision and Consuelo, on the outskirts of the city upon receiving a planned signal. As the Royal Azteca exited the palanquin, he wore a large smile on his face. His head was covered by a gold headpiece with large, feathered plumes displayed at the top. A gift of obsidian and gold knives was presented to the Tarascan emperor and his empress as they offered the Azteca leader a gold, silver and obsidian sword. The young daughter of this Tarascan ruler stepped up to who she thought was Dificil and bowed. She thought it was strange that the huge Timber Wolf Llore had not accompanied him, nor did she see any sign of the eagle Itta. The well-disguised Little Feather took her hand and walked with her, following the father, mother and the rest of the Tarascans into the temple. General Raton nervously followed alongside them. Upon entering this temple, the Aztecs were amazed at how huge it was inside. It didn't appear to be so large from the outside. The party began to walk down a steep stairway further into this royal chamber (or what seemed like a huge cavern). When they reached the lower-level platform, the interior appeared to be even larger than before. Suddenly, it was evident that a huge number of Tarascan warriors were stationed on their right and to the left! There had to be a few thousand at least! The Tarascan emperor, his empress and their young daughter suddenly disappeared in the horde of Tarascan warriors.

The Azteca Aguilas immediately surrounded Little Feather as the enemy began their attack! There was slashing and cutting, screaming and yelling as many Tarascan warriors began to fall.

Highly disciplined in all facets of "close order combat," the Aguilas continued their fierce fighting. They were like a machine! All as one, they fought! Slash and Stab! Shield and thrust! The horror could be seen in the eyes of the Tarascan enemy. Never had they encountered such fierce, animal-like fighting, such precision and uniform movements! Suddenly, Little Feather saw the outer walls of the great cavern open like huge doorways sliding upwards. They already were completely outnumbered, and now Little Feather could see more warriors coming at them through the doors opening on the sides! Where were the reinforcements? Where was Dificil, and was he alright? During the initial onslaught of the Tarascan enemy on the Aguilas, Little Feather had already received a telepathic message from Dificil that his men were just outside trying to get in! Had they been stopped, held off and killed? Just the thought made Little Feather more furious as he was taking down two warriors at a time! Heads were rolling, arms and legs were strewn in piles all around them as the killing and maiming continued! The Tarascans were concentrating their attack towards Little Feather! They were trying to get through all the Aguilas to strike him down! The Aguilas continued to try to maintain a circle around Little Feather. This was most difficult because he was moving so swiftly through the multitude of Tarascan warriors. He was like a ball of hot fury going through them and making a way towards the west wall! "Stay to your left, Aguilas! To your left! Don't let them steer you to the right," Little Feather continued to command. More Aguilas were now falling and dying! The Tarascans were too much in number. They kept coming and coming! It was beginning to become almost impossible to proceed forward because of all the bodies piling up! More and more Tarascan warriors were coming at them from both sides.

"I am here, Little Feather! I'm in the chamber and very close to you! Hold on my dear brother! Hold on! I'm almost by you!" Dificil kept yelling these words, and he kept sending the same urgent message through his telepathy! He too was slashing and cutting! Stabbing and slicing! Kicking, pushing, shoving, anything he could do to get through the huge number of enemy warriors between him and Little Feather! Dificil and his Aguilas had surprised the Tarascans and their allies who were stationed outside the temple! When they first saw the cloud of dust coming upon them, they did not immediately realize it was Dificil and thousands of Azteca reinforcements! The Tarascans thought that they had easily fooled the Azteca and that they would quickly annihilate them. As the Azteca proceeded towards the temple, more and more kept coming! Hundreds and thousands! The Tarascans screamed in fear and panic. As the Tarascan warriors tried to fight off the relentless attack of the Azteca Aguilas, they realized they could not stop them. "They are like devils with fire in their eyes and the wind at their backs! They seemed to be barking and growling like devilish dogs with each strike and killing!" "We are surely fighting a fiendish and supernatural foe!" This is what was going on in the minds of the Tarascans as they tried to fight back to no avail! Llore was ferociously attacking anything in front of Dificil. He came close several times to biting General Moztla, who was also valiantly trying to stay in front of Dificil. Itta could be seen repeatedly swooning down upon the enemy and swiping at them with his sharp talons and pecking at them with his equally sharp beak, decapitating and dismembering at least one Tarascan each time! As the bloody fighting continued, Little Feather could see that they were being cornered into the east side of the temple, and they could not move to their left! There was the enemy to their left, in front of them and at their rear! Now he could see a huge pool of water that was just before them in the center of the temple. "How could this be? Out of nowhere appeared this great body of water, and now they were being pushed towards it! "Dificil, Dificil! I fear I may not see you before they strike me down! I have failed in protecting you! I failed in defeating our enemy," Little Feather kept screaming these terrifying words over and over as the Aguilas continued to fall all around him! Suddenly, he felt a tear of sword at his left side! He felt a stab from a spear in his chest, and now he realized that some of the blood dripping from his chest, his arms and his legs was his blood! His guts and flesh!"

"Damn these filthy, evil vermin! I cannot let them kill me, for I must make sure that Dificil is safe first! Oh God of the Sun and of the Earth! God of Fire and War, please help me to stay alive long enough to protect Dificil, please, please," Little Feather yelled out as he continued to lash out at his enemies! These were the last words that Little Feather screamed as he valiantly continued to fight the Tarascans, even though he was mortally wounded. The blood now flowed profusely from all over his body, and he began to get weaker and weaker as he was at the edge of the great pool. He felt another stab in his chest, and an arrow pierced his right cheek. Little Feather fell headfirst into the water, and his body began to sink fast towards the bottom of the huge pool!

"I hear you Little Feather! Hold on my brother! Hold on, please," these words shrieked out from Dificil's mouth and from his mind. He looked to his left and could still see Consuelo. "We must cut through this horde of Tarascans! I fear we may not reach Little Feather in time to save him," Dificil yelled out to Consuelo. She like Dificil, was stabbing, slashing and cutting and trying to push forward, doing anything that she could to get through all the enemy warriors! She had heard the same telepathic message received from Little Feather. Somehow, she already knew it was too late! She could see General Moztla fighting and Llore right there with him, striking down the enemy. Dificil was moving through the enemy like a bolt of lightning. He was cutting down two or three warriors at a time! "Please, my Lord, let us stay in front of you and keep a circle around you! There are so many warriors, and it's hard to keep them away from you," exclaimed General Motzla. "No general! We must hurry, move faster! Little Feather is in grave danger! I must reach him before they can strike him down," answered Dificil. Finally, they had succeeded in driving through the enemy. The Azteca were now overtaking them, and it would not be much longer until they would completely defeat them! Suddenly, there seemed to be a clearing a short distance in front of them! "What was that?" The huge pool of water lay just ahead. There were bodies floating on its surface, and the water was not blue, but red from the blood of so many fallen warriors. Now the Tarascans and their allies were dropping their weapons and surrendering! All before him Dificil could see so many, many bodies, but where was Little Feather? As the Azteca Aguilas continued to round up and take many prisoners towards the outside, Consuelo along with many of Dificil's bodyguards proceeded to move forward. They struggled to step over all the bodies as Dificil had already instructed the Aguilas to hurry and search for Little Feather. Both Llore and Itta were ahead of Dificil and the Azteca warriors. They were using their great sense of smell trying to track the whereabouts of Little Feather!

"Little Feather! Little Feather! I'm here my brother! Where are you, Little Feather? Please, Little Feather, answer me! Where are you," Dificil repeatedly yelled out in desperation. Frantically, he continued to step over all the many corpses as he looked for Little Feather. The Aguilas continued to turn over the bodies lying on the ground before them to see if any one of them was Little Feather. Consuelo, with tears running down her face, stepped alongside Dificil with great fear that Little Feather was already dead! As they searched and searched for him, the Amazon Queen noticed Llore and Itta were in the huge pool going around in circles frantically trying to pick up his scent! She ordered her female warriors to dive into the water and help search for him. The Amazons were skilled in diving to great depths in the water, and as part of their training, they could hold their breath for a very long period before having to come back up to the surface. There was fury in the eyes of Dificil, but also great sadness. Where was Little Feather? Everyone around Dificil was horrified as he suddenly dropped to his knees! They thought he was injured! Consuelo immediately dropped to her knees next to him and screamed, "Are you hurt Dificil? What is wrong Dificil? Where are you hurt," screamed Consuelo. "It's not me who is hurt yelled Dificil, it's Little Feather! Help me find Little Feather," Dificil yelled out again in anguish. Dificil dropped his weapons and bowed his head in his hands and began to scream, "Little Feather! Little Feather! Answer me, Little Feather!"

Just then, a Tarascan warrior who was lying near Dificil suddenly rose to his feet with a sword in his hand and charged towards him! General Motzla was just a short distance to the side of Dificil and rushed to get in front of him. The Tarascan warrior lashed out with his sword at Dificil's head! General Motzla dove in front of Dificil and extended his arm with his sword to block the blow. He screamed out in agony as he saw his own right arm fall from his body to the ground. At the same instant, Consuelo swung her sword out at the Tarascan and immediately severed his head! Dificil rose to his feet, hearing General Motzla's screams and leaned over him and held him in his arms.

With the blood gushing out from his shoulder, General Motzla already began to lose consciousness. Dificil told Consuelo to retrieve his arm and bring it to him. As Dificil ran his hand over the head of General Motzla he said, "Oh my brave friend! You tried to sacrifice yourself in order to save me! May the Gods abundantly bless you, as I will not let you die?" As Consuelo handed the severed arm to Dificil he began a soft, slow chant and was beginning to place the arm in its original position, attached to General Moztla's shoulder! Dificil waved both his hands repeatedly over the area where the General's arm was cut off, and he continued to chant what seemed to be a strange prayer in a strange language. Suddenly, Consuelo noticed Dificil's eyes turned white, and they seemed to be rolling in his head! All his eyes were white! All of them were looking towards the heavens!

As Consuelo and Dificil's bodyguards looked on, they stared in wonderment as General Motzla now rose to his feet! His arm was back in place and there were no signs of any blood or of any wound! By the Gods! How was this possible? "How could Dificil reattach his arm? Truly Dificil was gifted with miraculous, supreme powers and he must indeed be a descendant of Quetzalcoatl," exclaimed Consuelo! After rising to his feet and having his arm reattached, General Motzla dropped to his knees in front of Dificil in awe, praise and gratitude! He put both his hands on Dificil's feet, began to lean forward and tried to kiss them.

"My Lord, you have saved me when it was I who attempted to save you! I praise your name, I kiss your feet, may all Azteca praise your name," General Moztla yelled out! "Please, my dear friend, rise. You need not praise me so, for I am here to save all my people and lead them to their true destiny! I am not a God, I am but your leader and friend," Dificil exclaimed as again he took hold of General Moztla and helped him to his feet. Consuelo too, began to rise to her feet as she continued to look upon Dificil in sheer love and amazement! As Dificil turned towards the great pool of water, he again yelled out, "Hurry, we must find Little Feather as quick as possible, for if he is injured, we must give him whatever attention he needs. Faster! Faster! I hope we are not too late! "Little Feather! Where are you! Little Feather, my brother, where are you!" With such blazing fury in his eyes and lightning-like pangs in his heart, Dificil yelled out, "Move, move, hurry, we must find him! We must find Little Feather!"

CHAPTER TWENTY-NINE
"ASSAULT ON THE MAGIC CITY"

As planned, the Tarascan warriors were assembled at the edge of the forests, just a few miles from the "Magic City" of the Azteca's Tenochtitlan. Intermingled with them were other enemies of the Azteca, including 10,000 Psiutes and 5,000 Huexotzingans. During their devious planning of the takeover of the Aztec empire, the traitorous Azteca General El Raton provided what he described as advantageous routes to the outskirts of the city. He had deviously devised this plan of surprising the Azteca with a major assault on Tenochtitlan while at the same time attempting to assassinate Dificil in the Tarascan city of Tzintzuntzan! He believed that this would be the ultimate means of totally defeating the Azteca and taking over their kingdom.

The enemy mistakenly marched as a single unit towards Tenochtitlan. Scouts had been dispatched the night before and tried to hide themselves along the perimeter of the Azteca city. Unbeknownst to them, the Azteca military was expecting them and watched as they placed themselves at various points.

It was so hot and so quiet! "Too quiet, he thought!" There wasn't even a wind or a soft breeze. "Xocoyotzin," (the smallest, "Little One") looked out from his battle placement. He was given this name at birth by his father. He was born a premature baby, so tiny, but miraculously he survived. Showing such strength, stamina and will to live, his father said he was little but as brave and strong as a man, thus his given name. He and his warriors were stationed at the entrance of Tenochtitlan directly behind the Azteca Otomie Aguilas. He intently watched for any kind of movement as he looked towards the east, which was the direction they expected the evil Tarascans and the other alien invaders to come from. Sweat poured from atop his head as he momentarily removed his headpiece. The armor bearer feared for his life but more for his master's.

As he wiped the neck and forehead of Xocoyotzin with a cool cloth, his hands shook so much that he told him to stop. This was their first taste of battle and such an important mission. Xocoyotzin commanded a full contingent of 5,000 elite Mayan warrior troops to assist Dificil's Aguilas in defending Tenochtitlan. His is father "Mochipa," the emperor of the Mayas had been saved through the kindness of Dificil years before when he was a captured prisoner, and because of that, he had told his son that he was indebted to Dificil. The Aguilas defending Tenochtitlan did not know of this until the night before due to the strict secrecy that Dificil and his father Chichinotpotol had ordered. When first hearing of the planned joining of the two nations, the Aguilas were shocked and a little apprehensive. Dificil himself met with all his Aguilas personally and assured them that there should be no doubt of the trustworthiness and loyalty of the Mayas.

Throughout history, the Azteca and Mayas often waged battle against each other mainly due to territorial disputes. Never were they known to agree on anything, let alone to unite and fight against a common enemy! Dificil had changed all that that day in the Aztec temple when he demonstrated such mercy and kindness to Mochipa and his surviving soldiers. No one knew of the secret meetings of the Azteca and the Mayas over the past couple of years. For the first time in the history of the world the Mayas were going to fight alongside the Aztecs instead of against them!

Xocoyotzin was young, just turning seventeen years old at the last full moon. He like Dificil, was being groomed as the heir to his father's throne. As was the tradition of the Azteca, he was required to engage in battle and prove his leadership skills, strength and courage and like Dificil, he began his training in all facets of military and martial arts at the young age of four years old. Today, he would make his father and his people proud! He was nervous but determined to demonstrate his valor, cunning and fighting skills! He had met with Dificil, Chichinotpotl, El Vision, Little Feather, General Moztla and Consuelo just the week before accompanying his father. He was astounded by the sight of Dificil, especially when he saw his eyes, all his eyes! He could not help but be captivated as he watched and listened to Dificil as he walked around and talked during their meeting. To him, it was like watching some strange god or something. He noticed a remarkable difference from Dificil to all other men, to all other humans! There was an aura of majesty and greatness about him, but also a true spirit of humility.

It was evident that Dificil was a gift of the gods, and Xocoyotzin remembered hearing stories about his prophesized arrival many times as he was growing up.

One week before the planned battle, Dificil ordered General Moztla to place Aguilas in the trees of the forest to watch and alert their comrades the moment the enemy began its trespass into their territory. Each Aguila assigned as a "lookout" was especially trained to withstand any kind of weather and to endure long periods without water or having to relieve themselves of their body waste. This was important to the Azteca just in case the enemy traveled to the forest and city perimeter days ahead of time. The Azteca lookouts were also trained to be able to stay completely still, perched in a tree, camouflaged so well that they were virtually invisible. Each Aguila that was stationed was in the possession of a falcon to be immediately dispatched by them to notify the Aguilas guarding Tenochtitlan of the first sight of any intruders.

The enemy scouts that arrived in the forest and along the perimeter of Tenochtitlan the night before the battle were being closely watched by the lookouts. The falcons had already been released and warned the defenders of Tenochtitlan. The Azteca were well prepared and anxious to do battle with the enemy.

Hundreds of the Azteca enemy raced towards Tenochtitlan, through the forest, across the plain and headed towards the interior of the city. As usual, the first line of defense for the Azteca were the elite Otomies. The two highest military societies or orders were the "Otontin "Otomies" and the "Cuauhchique, "Shorn Ones." They were the elite fighting force known to be the absolute best. Their heads were shaven except for a braid which would extend over their left ear. Their faces and heads were painted half blue and half red. Yellow would sometimes also be used. Each time before going into battle, the Shorn Ones would make a vow to never move backwards and if they did, they would be killed by their comrades.

The Azteca Otomie archers stretched their bows, arching high into the sky, as they aimed and released hundreds of poison arrows directly at the attacking Tarascans, Psiutes and Huexotzingans. The archers had been placed on either side of the valley leading into Tenochtitlan. There were so many arrows in the sky that it seemed as if the sun was blotted out, and suddenly it appeared to be nightfall! Piles and piles of the bodies of the enemy began to appear on the field of battle and the large force of enemy soldiers proceeded to move towards the city gates. As they marched on suddenly, another huge force of the Azteca Otomies sprang up from beneath the surface of the earth where they were hiding and stood between the Tarascans, Psuites and Hexotizingans and the great "Golden City." As the Otomie rose from the ground large clouds of dust formed and blinded the oncoming invaders. Screaming, grunting and barking like dogs, the Otomie attacked the troops that still advanced! 7,000 Otomie were in the front line defending their city and an additional 13,000 Shorn Ones, along with the Mayan troop accompaniment were lined up behind them to strike down any alien troops that somehow made it through the first lines of defense! Shield, stab and thrust! Shield, stab and thrust! Repeatedly was the motion and deadly action of Tenochtitlan's defenders! Slicing and stabbing! Ripping and tearing of flesh!

Xocoyotzin could not believe his eyes! Many of the Azteca had fallen dead and wounded as the enemy was still advancing to the city. He gave the order to attack as he and his troops joined with the Shorn Ones in making their fierce stand to protect

Tenochtitlan and the Aztec empire. His men were all around him as the bloody fighting raged on. Xocoyotzin now noticed that there were many more of the enemy than he thought! Everything now was just a blur of arms, swords, spears, arrows and heads flying! His men continued to try and stay in front of him, but to no avail. The attackers relentlessly kept coming and coming at them! All the prior apprehension and fear that Xocoyotzin may have had before the battle disappeared as he fought with everything he had in him! The Shorn ones in front were not backing up, but many, many of them were falling to the ground! How could this be? How is this possible! Xocoyotzin silently prayed to the war god Huitzilopochtli, "All magical and powerful Huitzilopochtli, please give me the strength and fighting skills to survive this fight. I am ready to die in honor, but I honestly would prefer to live!" Xocoyotzin now remembered the chill that ran through his body the night before when he had seen an owl perched above his tent! (The Azteca and Maya believed the owl to be a bad omen, signaling misfortune and death). Xocoyotzin fought fiercely back at what seemed to be a never-ending onslaught of the evil enemy! He repeatedly thrust with his obsidian sword and struck out with his club! Kicking, biting, knocking down and killing the enemy utilizing all his fighting skills! The battle scene was sheer madness and terror! Most of the Tarascans were armed with stabbing javelins and an "Atatl," (a long weapon used to throw a dart), and others struck at their opponents with obsidian-bladed clubs. Everywhere, all around him, his men and the Aztec Aguilas were courageously fighting! It was so "close order" that the enemy many times inadvertently struck one of their own while fighting an opponent! The Azteca and the Maya were a more disciplined fighting force and averted most of this happening amongst themselves.

Xocoyotzin now felt himself being pushed from the rear as the reinforced Azteca Aguilas furiously pushed forward, moving the enemy back. He noticed that his steps felt soft due to the water beneath his feet, for he was right at the edge of one of the water "causeways" leading into the city. This huge force of Azteca reinforcements knew they could not allow the enemy to get any closer to their city! The young Maya leader felt a spear enter his side as he struck down another Tarascan warrior. As he was fighting off still another, one of the Psuites stabbed him in his right leg with an obsidian knife, and he felt himself losing his balance! His soldiers tried to pick him up, but it was almost impossible because they were fighting and defending themselves against the enemy at the same time! He now felt the excruciating, icy pain of a blow to his head! Somehow, he heard the calling of his armor bearer, which seemed to be coming from afar off distance when he was right next to him!

"Xocoyotzin! Master! Master! Let me help you up! Oh, great gods help me save my master! Please help me take him from here and get him to safety!" His armor bearer struggled to pick him up and was now being helped by two Aguilas. An exit lane was provided as they transported the mortally wounded Xocoyotzin to the rear. His body was covered with so much blood from the numerous wounds he had received. As he was being carried to the rear lines, though almost blind from the sheer pain, he could tell that now the Aguilas were gaining momentum and were pushing the enemy back! It seemed that finally the invaders were falling back and losing the fierce battle!

The Tarascans and their cohorts planned to surprise the Azteca, but instead were shocked and surprised! With a victory, the enemy planned to enter the gates of the great city of Tenochtitlan, but instead they were being massacred by the Mayas and the Azteca Aguilas at what seemed now to be the "Gates of Hell!" They did not expect that Dificl had 20,000 additional Aguilas waiting for them at the front of the city! Horrid, terrible screams filled the air surrounding Tenochtitlan, and the soil was drenched with the blood of many warriors, and the water leading into Tenochtitlan's causeways began to turn red! Bodies began to pile on top of each other as the Aguilas tore the invaders to pieces. Though their losses were many, the Aguilas began their scream of, "Atl-tlachinalli! Atl-tlachinalli!" again the Aztec War Cry, proudly proclaiming their great victory!

CHAPTER THIRTY
VICTORY AND RESTITUTION!

With his father Chichinotpol at his side, and with the help of El Vision, Consuelo, Llore, the great eagle Itta and 1,000 of his bodyguards, Dificil continued to search for Little Feather. Through the fruitless search, the only thing they found at the foot of the pool was the gold jaguar bracelet that Dificil had given Little Feather. Only after Dificil had fallen from pure exhaustion and dehydration did he stop searching and let his father have the Aguilas take him home to Tenochtitlan. Even as he lay asleep on his bed of feathers and cloth, he kept saying repeatedly, "Little Feather, where are you?" Little Feather, come back to me, my dear brother! Please, where are you? Chichinotpotl allowed the Teopixque physicians to give Dificil some herbs mixed in "pulque" to help Dificil sleep, but he still did not sleep soundly. His body tossed and turned. His breathing was irregular, and a strange, animal-like growl was emanating from deep within his chest! Just as before, his mother, the Empress Cuicani, the senior Nana and Consuelo all sat together at his bedside, worrying and praying to the gods to restore him and make him better. The senior priest were just outside offering animal "Uemmana" (Nahuatl meaning sacrifices) and many, many prayers to the gods for Dificil's well-being.

After all the fighting was over and when they were still at the scene of battle, General Moztla and the Aguilas looked upon the many bodies of the enemy. Through their review of the fallen enemy, General Moztla discovered that Dificil and La Salvadera were right. They had said during the final war meeting that the other tribes joining the Tarascans would be Tlaxcalans and the Huexolzingans. The Aztecas were able to identify them by their war banners, the way their faces were painted and by their weapons. General Moztla had proceeded to round up all the members of the Tarascan royal family. He was successful in capturing the Tarascan ruler, his wife and daughter at the foot of the mountains along with the vile, treasonous General Raton. General Moztla had to force himself not to immediately decapitate El Raton or remove any of his body parts due to the strict orders of Dificil that he alone would personally send El Raton into the next life!

As Dificil lay in his restless slumber, he began to dream. Again, the "Cochitta," Once again, the recurring nightmare! "With the wind whistling in his hair, he stepped out from his teepee."

The brisk, fresh air flowed through his nostrils as he smiled, contented to live this great adventure, this life, another day!

As the new sun rose above the horizon, his eyes sparkled and were dazzled by its brightness.

All species of birds, fowl and insects were about him in abundance as he bowed his head to pray, "Oh glorious God of all life, Oh Lord of all being and reason, thank you for another chance to enjoy what you have set before us.

To the four corners of the earth, through the air, over the land and across the sea.

I will keep my covenant with you to respect all life, all the animals of whom I will speak, all the plants of whom I will nurture and cultivate and all the waterways which will cleanse me, quench my thirst and carry all sea life for me to eat!

The waves of the precious bison roam the grasslands and make the sounds of thunder upon the earth. I will, with due respect, hunt them for my food, to clothe myself and keep myself warm and shelter my lodge."

Suddenly, alarmingly, "What is that I smell and see?" The scent of "Death" and dark clouds appear, for with his arrival, he brings such horrible and deadly disease from the east!

A horrid, demon-like creature upon a dark horse cometh towards me!

He carries a sword of pestilence, he brandishes a lance of murder, treachery and deceit, and he spits from his foul mouth poison upon the crops and fields,

As he is a frightening, foreboding creature of no color!

Somehow, he is accompanied by other creatures bearing a Cross!

Who maim and kill in the name of their god!

They come on large boats that swim through the perilous seas to land and invade us here!

I shall prepare a new formidable shield to do battle against this coming strange foe!

I must hide my spouse and children within the great mountains, for as told eons ago, there will be no defense against this cruel intruder and his company will be as numerous as the filthy, ravenous weeds upon the land! Dificil saw "Huitzilopochitli" the Aztec Sun and War God. His eyes fluttered as he struggled to wake himself, and then he saw………..." Mictlantecuhtli!" The god of Death! But no wait! Someone moved Mictlantecuhtli away, and now he is standing there, extending his hand to Dificil! "Get up, my brother. Don't worry! Everything will be alright!"

Dificil suddenly woke up from his dream, sweating profusely and with a look of desperation on his face as he screamed, "Little Feather! Little Feather! Is that you? You're alive? Are you well? Somewhere, somehow, I must find you," he yelled. Everyone around Dificil at first was frightened, but then overjoyed as he awoke from his troubled slumber. They all stood still and silent as they listened to Dificil call out to Little Feather, and at the very same moment, the Aguilas were still searching for him or his body at the site of the battle. As Dificil awoke, his mama, the Senior Nana, and Consuelo all came to him and encircled him and wrapped him in their arms. "Stop, stop! You're suffocating me! You hold me so tight I cannot breathe," Dificil yelled out! As the three women stepped away from Dificil, they laughed at his words and relished in the joy that their Dificil was back with them again! As she adoringly looked upon her son, the great Empress Cuicani still saw her little boy in the body of what was now a man!

Cuicani, too, had dreams prior to Dificil's birth. She now looked at them not as dreams but as premonitions. Upon Dificil's birth, she already knew that he would be special, the prophesized prince that would save the Azteca empire. For years, when speaking of his historical birth, the teopixque forecast his special talents, his wisdom, his genius intellect, his deep, powerful compassion, and that he would possess a great amount of empathy and care for all humanity. Cuicani was told long before his birth by the senior Tlamatini that due to these heartfelt feelings, some would see this as a sign of weakness, but they would be sorely mistaken, and it would prove to be to the detriment of any of his foes. He had already, in his young life demonstrated how concerned he was about others and how tragedies would especially affect him. The teopixque told Cuicani that because of Dificil's godlike spirit, it would be expected of him to react this way; therefore, in his own mind and heart, he would always be devising ways of preventing any calamities or tragedies before they happened. Dificil would have the foresight and miraculous ability to see things that no one else could.

As Dificil looked up, he immediately saw El Vision at the door and, through their telepathy, told him they must see to their unfinished business. As he walked out to the corridor from his chamber, he smiled at his father, Chichinotpotl, and then General Moztla, a confident smile illustrating his renewed energy and strength. As always, everyone looked upon Dificil in wonderment! Set before them was not just a person, a human being, but someone who seemed so powerful, so resilient, so now, seemingly, supernatural! Now, even though he seemed physically refreshed, Dificil, of course, still was troubled by the mystery of Little Feather's disappearance. His heart ached, but he knew he must continue and finish the all-important task at hand.

As he was taught by his father, El Vision, and the Tlamatini, the vanquished enemy survivors must be shown the futility and fatalness of going against the Azteca! Accompanied by Chichinotpotl, El Vision, Consuelo, and the rest of the Aguilas, Dificil returned to the capitol city of the Tarascans, Tzintzuntzan. He immediately ordered that General Raton and all surviving enemy warriors be gathered and placed upon their knees in the center of the city to witness how he and his people would render punishment upon the traitor El Raton and his cohorts.

Dificil had already envisioned this scene of the burning city and the thousands of people before him in his dreams the night before. "Huitzilopochtli" had told him what he must do to ensure that his enemies would not forget what it would cost those who dared to go against his people. They must suffer death and annihilation! They must now know that they will always be below the Azteca and must pay homage and restitution!

El Raton was in front of Dificil on his knees! "You dared to believe you could fool the Azteca! You stupidly believed you were wiser than the great Chichinotpotl and I? You were for many years, entrusted with the honor to lead the Aguilas and wage war upon all our enemies, but now you chose to lie and dishonor our people. You chose to utilize your talents in deceit and treachery rather than with honor and the protection of my father and our empire! You have soiled the legacies of our

forefathers and have gone against the code of honor of all
Azteca! "Huitzilopochitli" has witnessed your devious,
venomous treachery and has ordered not only that you die but
that you suffer a slow death, a death befitting such a vile creature
as yourself."

El Raton, in chains and already bleeding from his mouth,
his nose, his head, and his ears from the beatings he had received
during the night, began screaming in horror at the feet of Dificil.

Looking at the rest of the vanquished Tarascan enemies,
Dificil said, "I command you all to look upon this foul waste!
Watch as I disembowel him and sever his genitals! Look closely
as I remove the hands and arms from his body that he used
against the Azteca. I will remove his legs and feet that he walked
on to make plans with our enemies. I will cut off his head and
place it upon a stake at the entrance to this city to remind
everyone of the consequences of betraying the Azteca."

Dificil proceeded with the execution of El Raton, slowly
and deliberately. All the surviving Tlaxcalans, the
Huexolzingans, and especially the Tarascans, looked on in
frightened horror! As Dificil severed each body part, many of the
people fell unconscious, as El Raton's screams were heard
throughout the valley and the surrounding mountains! Dificil
was filled with anger as he completed the execution on El Raton!
He ordered General Moztla to execute the Tarascan ruler and his
wife. Consuelo slowly and mercilessly slashed at her daughter
Fea, severing her into pieces! He also ordered the execution of
the leaders and council members of the Tlaxcalans and the
Huexolzingans. The surviving warriors were taken in chains to

Tenochtitlan to be imprisoned. As his ancestors before him, he decreed along with his father that the surviving citizenry of their enemies must be governed henceforth by a representative of the Azteca. They would forevermore be subject to Azteca rule and would be required to pay tribute to the Azteca, mostly in the form of monthly taxes. Dificil went back to the location at the foot of the mountains where his Azteca were camped and visited all his injured warriors and prayed at the graves of his fallen Aguilas, all the time wondering, where was Little Feather? Was he still alive?

"Little Feather, where are you? Are you hurt? Please answer me, Little Feather." Dificil called out through his telepathy, with all his heart and soul!

The sound of loud drums could be heard throughout the region. The conch horns blared their message of victory as the Azteca once again returned to their great city and celebrated their great triumph! "Atl-tlachinalli, Atl-tlachinalli," again the Azteca war cry! They jubilantly yelled out the name of their beloved Dificil! Dificil! Dificil! He had led them into battle! He led them to victory! He once again brought them glory! The news of the victory over the Tarascans, Tlaxcalans, and Huexolzingans preceded Dificil, his father, and the Azteca warriors upon their return to Tenochtitlan. They were greeted with beautiful flowers and reeds placed in front of them at every foot of the way. Young children's choirs sang praises as they triumphantly entered the city. At the top of the holy temples, priests were busy lighting great bonfires again with "Uemmana" to the gods to give thanks for such a great victory. As Dificil proudly walked alongside his father, thousands roared out their names. Difficil!

Chichinotpotl! Atl-tlachinalli! Walking behind Dificil were
Consuelo and La Salvadera. They were accompanied by El
Vision and General Moztla.

The Triple Alliance had been formally accepted and
preserved due to this triumph. Tlacopan, Tetzcoco, and
Tenochtitlan, the allied cities, divided the conquered land
amongst themselves. Dificil was proud and relieved with the
victorious outcome of their battle, but he was still with a heavy
heart, for he still had no idea of the circumstances of his brother,
Little Feather. Where could he be? What has happened to him?
The royal entourage made its way to the great pyramid of
Tenochtitlan. Dificil and Chichinotpotl walked up the steep
stairway to the twin temples of Tlaloc and Huitzilopochtli. Both
were such a creation of splendor and majesty. Tlaloc was painted
with the bright colors of blue and white, symbols of rain and
moisture. Huitzilopochtli was painted with red and white,
symbols of war and sacrifice. As in his dream, standing beside
his father, Dificil looked out upon "Anahuac," the valley of
Mexico. Below were all his subjects, thousands and thousands of
Aguilas calling out his name! As he was taught by the Tlamatini
and other priests during his training in the Calmecac, this same
place would be the site of his coronation, the fulfillment of the
prophecies. The great Dificil would be the next Tlatoani!
Throughout the rest of the day, seated atop the pyramid, Dificil
was entertained by dancers and magicians. Delicious, exotic food
was brought forth from many different regions. The Aguilas that
were responsible for testing the food and drink for possible
poisons were delighted by the wide variety of delicacies.
Beautiful Azteca maidens danced around him and placed

flowers, jade, rubies, silk, and gold laces at his feet, each one receiving a horrid look and growl from Consuelo as they passed her Dificil! As she sat just behind him, she looked upon his face, and her heart ached because she could see the look of sadness in all his eyes. Though others could not tell, she knew Dificil was not happy. She knew that Dificil was hurting a deep hurt, for he was heartbroken at the loss of his companion, Little Feather. She knew that he was just going through the motions and showing all manner of formalities and respect to all who were paying homage to him, but his real spirit was not there. Throughout the whole day and into the middle of the night, Dificil withstood all the ceremony and celebration. Many of the rulers of countries that were allies and others that were subject to the Azteca were allowed to pass in review of Dificil. They offered their well-wishes and bestowed many rich gifts upon him. Dificil shook his head in disgust as he looked at a few of the many that passed before him. He knew that some of these same people soon would be enemies of the Azteca as well. Such was their destiny; such would be the bad decisions they made, and as such, their ultimate demise!

Finally, when it was the early morn, Dificil rose and was escorted to his chambers to rest. He had fulfilled his royal duties and now needed so much to just be alone and rest. He was not only physically exhausted, but his whole being was drained. He needed sleep, and he needed quiet!

The Azteca celebration continued on for another week. The many ritual dances and ceremonies were performed in reverence to the gods. Many animals were sacrificed throughout these ceremonies. No human sacrifices were allowed because of the decree of Chichinotpotl, in following the wishes of his son, Dificil. The only human blood that was offered as sacrifice was that of the Tarascan ruler, his wife, his daughter, and, of course, the traitor El Raton. The head of El Raton, as was so ordered by Dificil, was placed on a stake at the entrance of the Tarascan capitol city, Tzintzuntzan. Dificil declared that all should see what the result would be for anyone becoming a traitor to the Azteca and conspiring against them. El Raton's feet were also placed on stakes at the entrance of the Tlaxcalan city and his hands were in turn placed at the center of the Huexolzingan capitol city. Word spread quickly throughout all of Mexico and Central and South America of how the Azteca had once again demonstrated their awesome power and invincibility in defeating a major enemy such as the Tarascans. Now more than ever, calpolli of many other lands learned of the Young Prince of Tenochtitlan Dificil and his great leadership and fighting prowess!

CHAPTER THIRTY-ONE
BURIALS & HEALING

It was the belief of the Aztecs that only the souls of those who died in particular ways found passage to the heavens, such as the spirits of the Aztec warriors who died in battle. Whether it was a dart piercing their neck, a dagger slicing their throat, or a spear or arrow running through their chest, their last breath escaping in desperation would wake them in the heaven presided over by Tonatiuh, an aspect of the sun god. They were joined by the souls of women who died during childbirth. The warriors that died in battle, the Aztecs believed, went directly into "Ilhuicatl," or "Tonatiuichan," (Sun Heaven). As Dificil looked out on the area where all his fallen Aguilas were buried, he noticed the monuments that had been hand-carved in the shape of a solar disk, the emblem of Tonatiuh.

An official honor guard composed of the elite "Otomie" and "Cuauhchique" Aztec warriors was assembled at the gravesite of the fallen warriors. They stood quietly at attention while the solemn sound of a drum roll could be heard repeatedly as Dificil stopped at each grave and offered prayers for each fallen Aguila. Hundreds of people looked on from a distance as the young prince paid homage to his soldiers. Again, his show of endearment and respect to his soldiers struck at the heart of not only the military but also all the citizenry of the Azteca nation. Never had any noble shown so much love for his people.

Xocoyotzin had fought valiantly on behalf of the Azteca in protecting their great city, Tenochtitlan. The Mayas thought of Dificil as someone very special and a descendant of the gods. Secretly, Dificil, Chichinotpotl, El Vision, and Little Feather had continued to meet with the Mayas. It was through these meetings that the Azteca gained important intelligence, and it was through this alliance that the Mayas refused to side with the Tarascans when asked to do so. They had told the Tarascans up front that they would never go against the Azteca.

The Mayas more than proved their commitment to the Azteca when Mochipa, the Mayan emperor, dispatched his son, the young prince Xocoyotzin, and 5,000 of his elite warriors to fight alongside the Azteca. After Xocoyotzin was carried to the rear when he was mortally wounded, the Teopixque physicians had diligently worked on his wounds to try and save him. When they had finished their final efforts in attending to his wounds, they thought the young prince was so seriously wounded that he would not survive.

When Dificil had returned from the battlefield, he was told of Xocoyotzin's grievous condition. He immediately went to the palace infirmary to see his young friend. Before he went up to the wounded warrior, one of the physicians told him that they had done everything they could for him, but his wounds were too serious for him to survive. Dificil knelt at his bedside and saw all the blood that covered his whole body. He felt so bad for the prince.

He then grabbed one of his hands and held it in both of his. "My dear friend, what has happened to you? I'm sorry I could not have been there next to you during the battle to save Tenochtitlan, but as you know, I had to be fighting off the evil demons in their own city at the same time. I must say our plans were successful, but at a great cost! Many of our brothers have fallen, and I wish that could have been prevented, but war is war!" Xocoyotzin could barely open his eyes when he looked at Dificil and said, "Oh, Dificil, it should not be necessary that you trouble yourself with my predicament. It is but my fate that I could not make it through the battle. I must say that I am proud to have served you and your father. I shall die with the happiness of knowing I helped stave off such a huge force of enemies. All praises to the gods that we were able to protect Tenochtitlan!" "No, my friend, thanks to the 'Great Spirit' for such brave souls like you and your courageous warriors!" Don't give up yet! I will not let you die!" Dificil then ordered everyone to leave the room. He then leaned over the injured prince, and with both his hands held over his wounded body, he began to hum and pray. He looked up to the heavens, and now his face beamed with light, and the light spread through his whole body, moving down to his arms and hands. Xocoyotzin, at the same time, began to experience a powerful trembling of his body, and then he felt a high degree of warmth all over him. The trembling increased to a feverish pitch as Dificil chanted some strange words over and over. Then Xocoyotzin felt himself falling unconscious, and days later, when he woke back home with his father, Mochipa, he would realize that he not only was still alive, but he had also healed from most of his serious wounds. Now in the care of his

Mayan physicians, he lay resting as his father and mother happily watched him with overflowing happiness and pride!

Examining him closely over and over, the Mayan physicians could not understand! They just could not believe how Xocoyotzin still survived after enduring such pain from his terrible wounds. They were amazed at how he was already healing so fast! Truly, the gods had to have performed a miracle on his behalf!

CHAPTER THIRTY TWO
"REST, SOLITUDE, WONDERING"

Dificil's mother, the empress Cuicani, his senior Nana; and all the rest of the Nanas were in the foyer of the temple awaiting Dificil when he arrived. As he entered the doors of the inner chamber, he just ran past them, threw his clothes off, and dove into the large, warm, volcanic pool. He sighed deeply as he felt the warm, soothing waters engulf his tired, sore body. As everyone looked on, he just slowly waded through the water, enjoying the feeling of just being able to relax. When Dificil had ran past everyone, Consuelo, who had accompanied him to the palace, just stood in the foyer as she watched him rush to the pool. His ever-present companion, Llore, followed him to the edge of the pool and just went down to a prone position and stood guard. Dificil's bodyguards were always amazed at how loyal and attentive Llore was to him all the time. He would leave his side only when Dificil ordered him to do so. The eagle was just above him, nearby, as always, watching! Dificil went from the volcanic pool to the other largest pool, where he relaxed some more and spent a little time playing with his dolphin friends. They too could tell Dificil was acting different, and part of him was not there. Dificil communicated to them that he missed Little Feather so much, and because of this, he was not feeling well. As the dolphins swam with him sand, as always, allowed Dificil to ride atop them, they tried to comfort him and engage him in their usual fun and games. Dificil only half-heartedly played along, constantly thinking of Little Feather. At least two hours had passed since Dificil first entered the pools, and now he was totally exhausted. As he exited the water, he lay on the large massage table that was next to the pool. The senior NaNa, after drying him, ordered the other younger NaNas to begin applying the different oils upon Dificil, and they began massaging his tired body. It was a good thing that Consuelo had retired into her own bed chambers and did not see the young NaNas touching Dificil. Even though this was the usual task that was performed by them regularly, they were careful and apprehensive now since Consuelo was part of the royal inner circle. The total love, dedication, and caring that she displayed for Dificil was obvious to all, and because of that, no one other than Chichinotpotl, his mother Cuicani, and ElVision would dare touch or get close to Dificil when she was present. All females knew that it would be very precarious to their health if they came near Dificil in front of her.

As Dificil lay on the table being administered to by the NaNas, he began to realize that he had come a long way. He could remember being just a small child when he first saw the sacrifices. He ran up the pyramid, shouting and yelling, and made the priest stop the killing! Then he remembered the arrival of El Vision and Little Feather. How quickly and naturally they bonded. The first journeys together in the forests, visiting with all the many different animals and his friend, the jaguar! He remembered the first day at the Calmecac, learning and listening to the Tlamatini and others. He and Little Feather discovered that they knew more about many subjects than the Teopixque but did not say so, and they were able to easily analyze the elements and the waterways presented to them in their studies of meteorological science and geography. Dificil, of course, remembered his first meeting with Consuelo, the Amazon queen, and how they instantly fell in love and became inseparable.

Together, he and Little Feather began their journey at a very young age. Why, they were just young boys eager to learn, to experience, and to dare the perils of life! In just a short time together, they changed the world, and they lived a life filled with excitement and adventure! But now what has happened to Little Feather? Is he dead?

The empress Cuicani was seated beside the table as she watched everyone trying to comfort and console Dificil. Her son was always more than kind to everyone and always very generous in giving gifts to all those around him. In the past, he always engaged in deep conversation with his NaNas, with his father Chichinotpotl, with her and El Vision, and especially with Little Feather. Now he just stood motionless, somber, and silent. When she looked into his eyes, all his eyes, she no longer saw that fire, that excitement, and that energy. She saw only a dark sadness, no life. She could see that Dificil was near sleep. She grabbed his hand and said, "Philli, Hualmonochilia, Huaomonochilia Dificil, Huamonochilianohuan." In Philli, Mochehuia (Nahuatl meaning, "Come with me, my son, and rest"). Slowly Dificil rose from the table and followed his mother to his bed chambers. He softly rubbed the head of Llore as the wolf followed alongside. The hallway leading to his chambers seemed to be so dark, sullen, and very humid.

The air seemed to be thick and suffocating, and there was complete silence as Dificil entered his room. He lay down with his mother and the senior NaNa at his bedside, and he began to close his eyes. When he started to drift off into a deep sleep, both his mother and the senior NaNa looked at him with such love and yet worry. Especially since Dificil began to talk in his sleep, speaking a strange, different language. The language was "Quiche," the language of the Mayas. Listening closely was also El Vision. He immediately recognized the language that Dificil was speaking. Dificil stopped talking in his sleep, and then he began to rest more comfortably.

Candles that were all around his bed were extinguished, and everyone left the room. Only a few of his personal bodyguards and El Vision remained. His faithful friend, Llore, was prone and alert at the foot of his bed, as the eagle Itta stood watch, perched on a rafter above. His breathing began to be rapid and hollow. His body began to tremble, and he began to moan, but then suddenly he lay completely still. His breathing returned to normal, and his whole body relaxed. Dificil stopped moaning as he felt someone holding his right hand. He felt another warm hand upon his forehead, and he felt the warm, exotic breath of Consuelo upon his face! Consuelo had just entered his bedchamber after being summoned by Dificil's mother, Cuicani. Cuicani was so distraught and sad when she begged the young Amazon queen to come and try to comfort her son. When Consuelo had entered the bed chambers of Dificil, she was accompanied by four of her Amazon bodyguards; they were there to assist her in comforting her beloved Dificil. They all sat opposite Dificil's bed.

Two of them began humming a strange but pleasant song, while the other two began playing their wooden flutes. Suddenly, an air of surreal peace and tranquility filled the room. Even Llore could be heard purring, and for once he seemed relaxed. As the Amazon maidens continued their soothing music, Consuelo wrapped her arms around Dificil and softly sang in his ear the ancient "Cuicatl" (Nahuatl word for song). As she sang, her lips were so close to Dificil that she kissed his earlobes. The song that she sang was of love and healing. She sang the song with all her being, and she sang with all her heart for her Dificil! Tears welled in her eyes as she dreaded the suffering that Dificil was enduring. She wished somehow that the gods would allow her to suffer in his stead and let her absorb all pain for him.

"Ma xipatinemi, Ma xipatinemi, Dificil. (Nahuatl meaning, "May you be well"). Sleep and rest, my dear one. Sleep and rest for the morrow brings freshness and new life! My heart is in your hand! My spirit is within your host, and my life is yours! Look all around you and fear no one, for I am with you even until the end of the world. I will never let any harm come to you. I shall wrestle the clouds down from the sky for you to rest your weary head. I will direct the moon to light your way in the night, and I will beckon the sun to brighten your day, and you will be safe and secure, for my arms will be wrapped around you. They shall comfort you and keep you warm, and you will not thirst, for my moist lips will be pressed upon yours!"

Consuelo sang, and she sang. She hummed, and she prayed to the gods for Dificil's soul. Her song was soft and sincere. Her song was for him, of him, and.................... Suddenly, Dificil sat up! He looked up at Consuelo, and he smiled! He wrapped his arms around her, and their lips met, and their bodies touched! Fire! Thunder! A Hurricane! Something not of this world had taken hold of Dificil and Consuelo as they felt each other's love! Spontaneously, everyone in the room quickly left. They knew that this was a special time. A special happening decreed only by the Gods! Now alone, Dificil and Consuelo held each other tight as if something or somebody would break them loose! With urgency never felt by either one, they ripped off each other's clothes. Each nerve in his body told Dificil that this was meant to be. As he felt Consuelo's lips upon his, his whole body was on fire! With shaking hands, his fingers touched her exquisitely soft "baby skin."

He touched the length of her strong arms, and he caressed her long legs, slowly beginning from her ankles to her preciously silky thighs. She laughed as Dificil squeezed her feet and said she had toes like those of a koala bear as she pinched him with those cold toes! He moved away from her only slightly as he placed his hands upon her full breast, and he squeezed. Now Dificil realized even more how special this creature lying with him was. This exotic Amazon queen, who was born in a rain forest, as foretold, had arrived here, joining with him and touching his very soul! Such a fierce warrior, but also a goddess from the heavens sent to him! They caressed, they touched, they squeezed, and they clutched. Consuelo was consumed by the same fire that raged in Dificil, and she felt the need to hold him and to possess him and her body to be part of his body! She felt his strength, his big, muscular legs, arms, and chest. She pulled Dificil back on top of her. How many days and nights did she think? Did she dream of being like this alone with her Dificil?

She felt his chest upon her breast. She wrapped her legs around him, and then she discovered what all the young NaNas had been talking about. She gasped in fear at the sight of him, but then moaned in delight as they joined together! All the stars in the galaxies appeared and disappeared! The moon and the sun flew by, and the mountains crumbled to the sea! He was part of her, and she was dificil, and together they were as one!

Chapter Thirty-Three
"Remorse, Acceptance, Revelation"

Long days turned into weeks, and slow-moving weeks turned into months, and still Dificil was in seclusion. Each day was spent at first in the pools, as he tried to relax, but all it did was remind him of how he and Little Feather used to laugh and play together with the Dolphins. By noon each day, Dificil could be found in the temple praying, praying for Little Feather's safe return.

The Tlamatini and all the rest of the priests would look on sadly at Dificil, so heartbroken and in so much despair. Every other day, accompanied by his bodyguards, Dificil would span the area of their battle over and over again in search of Little Feather. As the eagle soared above and Llore was at his feet, Dificil returned home each day disappointed. What happened to Little Feather? Where was he? Consuelo was always at his side as was El Vision. They tried to comfort Dificil and help him accept the terrible loss. El Vision reminded Dificil, "Little Feather, my beloved son, knew the dangers and accepted the possibility of dying in battle. It was his mission in life to protect you. May I say Dificil, he accepted this, and now you should accept it. I understand your sadness and bereavement, but you have been chosen by the Gods, and must continue with your mission and lead your people and your country. "Tezcatlipoca", the most powerful, supreme Aztec deity, associated with destiny and fate, has written and formulated your future, concluded El Vision. "As always my dear friend, your words are true and I accept my task, my destiny, but no words can ease the hurt and pain in my heart! I cannot and will not accept that Little Feather is gone forever," Dificil declared. Each evening upon returning to the palace, accompanied by Consuelo, Dificil would just go back into his personal chambers. Consuelo would return to her own quarters, unable to console Dificil. The Empress, Cuicani, the Senior NaNa, La Salvadera and of course, his father Chichinotpotl all tried to get Dificil out of his misery.

They tried to engage him in conversations. They brought him all kinds of delicious food and fruit from many different lands. Dancers, magicians, musicians, and many other different types of performers were summoned for his entertainment, only to be turned away. Then one day Consuelo realized that maybe there was something to revive Dificil's good spirits and bring some joy back into his life. She remembered he had told her of a very special place that even Little Feather did not know about! A place that seemed to be a haven for the Gods! This place, Dificil told her he had discovered all by himself. A place where there was serenity, peace, happiness and magic! A place where he said he had some friends. She remembered he had mentioned that it was located on the other side of the "Thorn-tree-place." This is where they would go. This is where they needed to go to bring Dificil back to the world, to the Azteca, to her! Consuelo went to speak with El Vision. She told him of this secret place of

Dificil's, and she told him that she felt that this could be the best method of healing him. Agreeing with her, El Vision then informed Emperor Chichinotpotl. The Emperor agreed but instructed El Vision that Consuelo must convince Dificil that he had to be accompanied by his bodyguards.

As agreed upon and planned, that same evening Consuelo met with Dificil in his private chambers. "Dificil, you told me about a special place that you have kept secret for years. You told me that one day you would take me to see it and experience its magic with you. I love you my dear Dificil and you know I, like the rest of your family, are worried about you. You barely talk to anyone. You hardly eat or sleep because of your great sadness and depression. Please, please Dificil, let us go now. You need to relax, to rest and to rejuvenate yourself. What better place to make this happen than your special place? When the sun comes up upon the horizon, let us leave and go to this place. I want to see it, to enjoy it with you," Consuelo exclaimed. Dificil listened to her request. He seemed to be in deep thought and he had a faraway look in his eyes, all his eyes, and as numerous times in the past, he began a soft, slow chant. He raised both his hands above his head and began to pray. His prayers were different. He did not chant songs to the usual series of gods but seemed to be speaking to only one god! His prayers were spoken in an unknown, strange language. After a while, he stopped praying, dropped his hands to his side, and then went and lay on his bed. Consuelo followed him and lay next to him. She rubbed her soft hands upon his forehead and began to sing a song. She sang softly and tenderly.

"The moon and the stars light your way at night.

Each day the sun shines upon you and warms you at first light, And the birds sing happy songs of praise to you!

Walk in the light my dear one, and gaze upon the clear, blue sky.

Be happy, so together we may listen and join the winged creatures, that fly, high above, In melodies of peace, harmony and love!"

Dificil turned towards Consuelo and held her close in his arms. She felt his pain and squeezed him even tighter and together they slowly drifted off into a peaceful sleep.

CHAPTER THIRTY-FOUR
"A SPECIAL MESSENGER"

Dificil woke up in the morning feeling refreshed and hungry. As he left his bed chambers, he sent word to his mother and father that he had something to talk to them about and would like to discuss this over the morning meal. Receiving word of their son's rejuvenation, both Chichinotpotl and the Empress Cuicani hurried to meet Dificil in the Dining Chambers. As his parents looked on happily, Dificil was eating everything in sight! They had not seen him with such a big appetite in a long time! Surely, he must be feeling better. Finally finishing the last few morsels of food, he began to speak to his parents.

"My dearest mother and father, I know you have been concerned about my health and well-being, and I know that it has been a long time since things have seemed to be normal around me. Of course, you know the deep hurt and pain that I have been feeling since the disappearance of Little Feather. I must tell you now that it is because of your most kind patience and love that I have been able to endure such sadness and grief. Last night Consuelo reminded me of a special place that only I know about. When she brought this to my attention, it made me feel hopeful and alive again! I wish to travel to this place immediately, and with your permission, I would only like to take El Vision and Consuelo with me. I would prefer Father not to have to take a whole battalion of Aguilas with me," Dificil concluded. "My dear son, if this place is as wonderful as you say it is, I see no harm in you traveling there. If this will help heal your spirit and provide you with a renewed outlook on your young life, I'm sure your mother and I are much in favor of such an excursion. I must insist, though, that when you embark on this journey, you be escorted by the eagle and jaguar warriors. As you know, no region is completely safe from potential enemies, my precious son," Chichinotpotl said. "Very well, Father, if it is your sincere wish that I be fully escorted, then I will obey."

Just then Dificil received a flash message through his mental telepathy from La Salvadera. The Mayan ruler that Dificil had befriended and shown so much kindness to that first day in the Calmecac had just arrived with an important message for Dificil and Chichinotpotl! La Salvadera now entered the palace and asked for permission to speak to Chichinotpotl and Dificil. She appeared to be stunned and greatly excited. "My dear Lords, I have just received word that the Mayan ruler is at the entrance of the royal chambers and wishes to have an audience with you. He says he brings exciting news from the shores of the great sea!" "Glory to Tenoch that such news is brought by our friend, the Mayan leader himself!" "Send him in immediately," commanded Chichinotpotl. The great doors to the royal palace opened as the Mayan leader and his military escort entered, dressed in their most formal attire.

"Panoltia, Panoltia, tlatohque!" Welcome, dear noble one," Chichinotpotl greeted the Mayan ruler. It has been many moons since we last were able to share a meal together. Please come and join us in eating some fruits and delicacies. I imagine your journey was very strenuous, and you must be hungry." Immediately all the servants and attendants were serving more food and refreshments for the Mayan and his entourage.

"You honor us with your visit, and I hope you bring good medicine here today," exclaimed Chichinotpotl. As the Mayan accepted the rich foods and spirits from the Azteca, he began to speak: "First of all, let me say that it is I who am honored to be in your presence once again. I now look upon our most recent united victory against the evil Tarascans and their cohorts as not only a great mission accomplished together but also a historical event that will be spoken of down through the ages. Dificil, no words could describe my gratitude to you once again for helping with the recovery of my son Xocoyotzin. Though his battle wounds were most grievous, you somehow healed him. Because of your kind, miraculous attention to his injuries, he was not only able to survive, but he did not lose a limb, his sight, or his ability to function as a normal human being!" Mochipa bowed before Dificil and his father and continued, "Allow me to present you with a few gifts that I had made especially in your honor. At that moment, several of the Mayan warriors stepped forward bearing gifts. Reaching over to one of the men, Mochipa was handed a golden spear with precious rubies along its base. The point of the spear was sculptured in the image of the war god Tezcatlipoca. A second gift was brought forth, which was an elaborate, beautiful headdress. It was of multi-colors and composed of the quills and feathers of many exotic birds. A third gift presented to Dificil was a wicker frame created as a protective canopy for his royal throne.

Both Chichinotpotl and Dificil stood in awe at such exotic gifts. "My dear friend, it is not necessary that you have presented me with all these wonderful gifts! Your friendship and assistance in our time of need was more than enough of a blessing from you, your son Xocoyotzin, and your people," Dificil declared. Chichinotpotl agreed and added, "I must say that your son demonstrated such great valor and courage of the highest order! His bravery and sacrifice will always be appreciated and remembered by our people!"

With that, Mochipa began his deliverance of a most important and shocking revelation: "I felt it most necessary to come in person with this news. I will never forget the kindness that you showed me that day at the Calmecac, when I was so wounded, hurt, and at your mercy. As we have communicated for many months, we will always be friends. My people, the Maya, are proud to be in alliance with you!

What I came to tell you is that my soldiers were patrolling as usual the shoreline of the southern waters. Four moons have passed since they discovered some foreign aliens who landed on our shores. They appeared to be dark in color and filthy! There were others with them who looked like priests. They wore long robes, and they had no hair upon their heads! As they landed, my soldiers confronted them. These strange-looking creatures began speaking in an unintelligible, foul-sounding language. They wore horrible-looking clothes upon their bodies, and my men stated that they smelled worse than a dead mountain goat! After much effort, my men, using hand signals, were finally able to communicate to these foreigners that they were not welcome and had to leave. Then the strangers instead tried to proceed further into our kingdom by force. They began attacking my soldiers without provocation.

My troops, in defending themselves, noticed these alien creatures bore very strange-looking weapons. One of the weapons they used spit fire, which made a round hole in the bodies of some of my men and killed them. Both landing parties displayed some of the same weapons. My men were able to beat both invading groups off and killed most of them. A few in both locations were able to escape and returned to their huge floating vessels. Upon examining the bodies of these strange men, my officers discovered that they all had large holes in their skin and pus-like sores all about their bodies. They all seemed to be undernourished, and most of them had very few teeth, which were black and rotten! I ordered my people to burn their bodies to prevent any of the sickness they had from spreading to our people. They truly seemed to be evil creatures sent from death and the underworld!"

Upon hearing this shocking revelation from Mochipa, Chichinotpotl, El Vision, and Consuelo looked at Dificil with a stunning realization! These were the same invaders that Dificil described in his recurring Cochitta! They thought his dreams or visions were something that would happen deep into the distant future. Now with this report of their landing on these very shores, it was apparent that these strange, evil invaders were real, and there was no doubt they would be returning very soon!

After dining with Mochipa, they all said their good-byes, and he departed back to his land. Dificil knew that he and his people must indeed prepare for this imminent danger and this forthcoming invasion! He and his father examined the objects that the Mayas captured from the invaders and were given to him by Mochipa. One was a heavy headpiece made of some strange hard material that their arrows could not easily pierce, and another, an object of worship made of gold, with one piece crossing the other.

Upon completion of their meeting with Mochipa and the terrible revelation of the strange visitors, Dificil again told his father of his wish to go on his special journey. Only after stern insistence from his father did Dificil agree to have his bodyguards accompany him and Consuelo on their excursion. So as not to stir too many curiosities, the Aguilas did not carry their usual banners or bring their weapon bearers with them. Everyone just thought that Dificil and his entourage were going to a place nearby that was in conjunction with the Nemontemi festivities. Consuelo had returned to her own bed chambers in the middle of the night, being that she and Dificil were not yet officially joined and blessed in matrimony. She just woke up and was being attended to by the other Amazons when suddenly Dificil walked into her chambers.

"I thought that the extinct volcano would have to miraculously erupt to awaken you! What are you waiting for? You insisted on going on this journey, so let us leave now! Consuelo was filled with joy hearing these words from Dificil and then proceeded to walk with him outside. She was awed at the sight of all the Aguilas dressed in their beautiful, green armor and the bright plumes atop their headdresses. This was the uniform of the elite "Jaguar" unit assigned as special bodyguards to Dificil. 'Twas just daybreak, and fortunately there was not the usual huge crowd of Azteca merchants and shoppers present in the center of Tecnochtitlan, but nonetheless, the Amazon Queen, as usual, cautiously looked all around to be sure that there were no signs of danger. The Azteca that were in front of the palace were surprised to see Dificil since he had not appeared in public for months. Bowing to him on their knees, they happily shouted praises and said prayers to the gods for him. The sun shone brightly, and there seemed to be a new freshness in the air. As usual, Llore walked alongside Dificil as the great eagle soared high above and El Vision followed right behind him and Consuelo. Consuelo looked upon Dificil's face and was filled with renewed hope because she did not see him smile, but he no longer had the look of gloom and despair in his eyes. Dificil walked with confident, long strides and had refused to be carried in the royal palanquin.

Chichinotpotl and his wife, the Empress Cuicani, had agreed not to accompany Dificil on his own private adventure, as General Moztla proudly led the way. Their journey took all of the day, and they rested the first night. As the Aguilas stood guard, they were amazed at how so many different animals stood nearby Dificil's camp. They even saw the feared jaguar pass close to their fires numerous times during the night. Dificil had told them not to worry since the jaguar was one of the closest of all his animal friends. With morning's break, the entourage moved on. They traveled an unfamiliar route that Dificil had described to General Moztla. Apprehensive and confused at first, General Moztla followed the directions of Dificil. This passageway was unknown to him or any of the Aguilas and thus was not drawn on any of their maps. They walked through deep forests, many shallow ravines, and around numerous mountain passes. As they continued, General Moztla was amazed at how, unless you knew of these pathways and mountain tunnels, you would never be able to see or find such natural, hidden paths. Just before dusk, they arrived at the foot of Mt. Huixachtlan, the site of the great volcano. It was astounding to the General that they had reached their destination in less than half the time it normally would have taken. Dificil called General Moztla and El Vision over to him as the royal caravan came to a stop.

CHAPTER THIRTY-FIVE
"A SPECIAL PLACE"

"We are there! Just beyond the rock and sand that you see ahead of us is an oasis. At the site of the oasis, I would ask that the Aguilas stand back and await my return. Only you and El Vision will accompany Consuelo and me there. Know that my words are sure and true, and you need not fear that there would be any danger for me in this special place. Llore and the Itta are already inside and have communicated to me that, as expected, all is well and safe. When you accompany me, you will see things that may be beyond your belief and understanding. This is why it is such a sacred and special place! Upon entering, you will immediately notice a wonderful, complete transformation of your body, mind & spirit. You must never, ever, reveal what you are about to see and witness. You must take this knowledge with you to your grave! Will you comply with my wishes?" Dificil asked. Bowing and exclaiming their service to their great Dificil, both General Moztla and El Vision vowed to secrecy as they followed him and Consuelo into the entrance of the oasis. At a point no one else could see, just a few feet away from where they had stopped, behind a roll of pine trees and at the foot of the volcano was the entrance to the oasis.

Hesitating, both El Vision and General Moztla just stood still in front of the trees. At first General Moztla did not see

anything that looked like an entrance. El Vision, who could not
see, just listened and let his mind and spirit guide him. As
General Moztla watched, El Vision suddenly took two steps
forward. Seeing this, Moztla could not believe his eyes when he
observed that El Vision's body was slowly disappearing as he
took more steps forward. "Do not be afraid, General Moztla;
what you are seeing is the reality of a secret dimension, another
part of our world no one else knows about. "Step forward and
you too will enter this 'Special Place of Happiness,'" exclaimed
Dificil. Looking back at Dificil, General Moztla, gingerly,
slowly, began to step forward. Holding his arms and hands up,
he too saw himself beginning to disappear in thin air! Suddenly,
he felt a great calmness, peace, and complete happiness! Taking
Dificil's hand, Consuelo followed him into the entrance of the
oasis. She marveled at the sudden transformation of not only
herself but also of everything all around them. All the plants,
flowers, and all the vegetation looked to be twice the normal
size. There was almost complete silence, yet one could hear the
melodic sound of singing birds and the echoing sound of water
rushing down a nearby waterfall. A calm, soothing wind rustled
Consuelo's long hair, and moistness from trees above settled on
her soft, smooth, silky skin. As everyone looked in front of them
at the beautiful waterfall just a few feet ahead, they could see
Llore and the Great Eagle seated on a cliff, surrounded by many
other animals. There were multi-colored parrots and swans and
huge, strange creatures with giant ears and long trunks
protruding from their heads. They saw very, very tall creatures
with long legs and dark spots on their skin trudging along in
front of them. They also saw all sorts of insects and snakes

crawling past them. Such beauty, such splendor, and so full of life! As if planned, General Moztla and El Vision asked at the same time, "Is this Aztlan?" Consuelo felt even more at home here in this strange, wonderful place, for it reminded her of her birthplace, just like a rainforest! There was a wonderful, heavenly scent about everything. The smell of wildflowers, limes, lemons, apples, greens, and fresh water. As they stepped further forward, everyone noticed large pools of water filled with exotic fish of many different colors and sizes. When they looked up, they could see many different ape-like creatures swinging from the branches and playing. Consuelo noticed one bear that Dificil had told her about. It had toes like hers, the koala bear, quite a furry type of creature with small, brown eyes and a little beacon of a nose. Several elegantly colored butterflies perched themselves upon Consuelo's hair. A couple of bright blue robins came up to Consuelo, and they too flew atop her head and placed a beautiful array of flowers in her lovely brown hair.

Suddenly, there was such a roar like thunder. The ground shook as if it was the beginning of an earthquake, and everyone looked in front of them from where the sound was coming. Now a large group of strange, beautiful four-legged creatures were running around the bend of the waterfall and down towards Dificil and his friends. Each animal was sleek and yet very muscular, with a long mane of hair hanging from their heads. They had large hooves, which were semi-rounded and made such a loud pounding sound upon the earth as they continued towards them. Most were shiny and pitch black in color. Others were brown, and a few were spotted with shades of black and white. Some smaller ones, which appeared to be babies, followed them.

As they reached the base of the hill and the waterfall, they suddenly stopped in front of Dificil and his friends. They stood still, breathing heavily, and were all looking up towards the location from whence they came. Again, there was the sudden sound of another animal coming around the hill. Looking towards the direction of the sound, there was a blinding brightness, and everyone could not help but squint as they tried to focus on the sight. There, out of nowhere, appeared the most beautiful, awesome-looking animal that anyone had ever seen! He was colored all white, so white that he was almost silver! He ran down the hill and stopped in front of Dificil and went down to one knee and bowed his head! Everyone but Dificil gasped and was shocked at what they now saw! It looked like a silver horn protruding from the front of his head! "Do not fear, my dear friends! He is a "unicorn," a most special friend and animal that will be written about until the end of time. These other similar-looking animals are "horses." They will prove to be very useful in the future. They will serve us in cultivating our land, they will transport us, and they will most importantly serve us in war! Indeed, in the future people will write of us and claim that we never had such animals, and yet they will lie from simple ignorance of not knowing the real history of our people."

The unicorn rose to his feet and bowed again to Dificil as Consuelo bravely ran her hand across his long mane. Dificil climbed atop the unicorn and grabbed Consuelo, lifting her up to sit behind him. "Wait here, General Moztla and El Vision. We are going to ride just a little distance from here with the unicorn. Again, I remind you that there is nothing to fear. Just wait and we will return in a little while. You may pick some of the fruit from the trees and bushes you see all around us. Their taste will be like nothing you have ever tasted before! Enjoy and relax, for I feel that good tidings are upon us!"

Both General Moztla and El Vision smiled with great happiness as Dificil rode away with Consuelo, and all the animals followed behind them closely. As they rode together in the bright sun, Dificil and Consuelo felt as one with each other and with all the lovely creatures that surrounded them. A huge rainbow could be seen by them both on the horizon as they rode forward. The rainbow reflected beautiful, glorious, heavenly colors! At the end of the rainbow, Dificil could see a gigantic Aztec warrior headdress, with golden plumes and white, red, and green feathers. He remembered now that he had seen this same thing many times before in his "Cochitta," his recurring dream. Dificil felt a resurgence of energy now. He had a feeling of renewed hope and encouragement! Sitting behind Dificil upon the Unicorn, Consuelo hugged him tightly with both arms and placed her head upon his shoulders! She never felt so sure, so safe, and so happy in her life! Llore ran alongside with the other animals and was grunting and barking loudly! Dificil knew that sound was a sound of happiness.

Just then a hawk could be seen above as he arrived atop a tree limb next to a dove. As he landed, the dove sprang from the branch into the clear blue sky and merged with a pheasant in full flight. The colorful pheasant then swooned down closer to earth and then glided over to Itta! As each beautiful bird crossed the path of the other, they seemed to be relaying an important, urgent message! Riding atop the unicorn, Dificil noticed how he suddenly began to slow down, and his head was pointed towards the sky. Dificil and Consuelo looked up now as Itta was flying above them. He was chirping rapidly and screaming! Not a sound he usually screamed out while he was hunting or during war, but a resonant, joyous sound! He now was flying in circles overhead and then flying upside down.

What was that he was saying? The white unicorn stopped, and as Dificil and Consuelo strained to hear, to understand what Itta was saying, Dificil yelled out, "Come down here, you crazy bird! Talk to me! Come closer so we can hear you!"

Still flying overhead Itta again was crying out the telepathic message he was sending! "What are you trying to say? Am I hearing what I am hearing or just what I want to hear?

What? What about Little Feather...?"

"LITTLE FEATHER! HE LIVES!"

Then Dificil once again raised both his hands to the sky and began to pray, "Thank you, Lord! Oh, thank you, wonderful Great Spirit! May the heavens praise you and sound out your glorious name!

THE END!!!

www.ingramcontent.com/pod-product-compliance
Lightning Source LLC
Chambersburg PA
CBHW060403310726
48976CB00003B/930